Project Hybrid 1

Project Hybrid

Project Hybrid 2

ISBN: 978-0-9850606-0-2

ACKNOWLEDGMENT

Special thanks go out to those that inspired me to write this book and kept me motivated throughout the process. To my Mother, Father, and Charlie for all the support and help to get to the final edit. To Mary and Kristina for inspiring the actions of the characters, and to Jordan and Alicia for motivating me to start this in the first place. And to everyone else that kept me motivated throughout it all. Thanks everyone. ☺

Questions without Answers

"BORN IN DARKNESS, RAISED IN LIGHT. TRAPPED FOREVER, IN A NEVER-ENDING TWILIGHT."

That's a line I'm all too familiar with. The memories are all a blur, but without warning, these visions from the past, or at least what I think is the past, come flooding into my mind, reminding me of my true purpose for existence. Hybrid. Project Hybrid. Every image, every vision, every memory is somehow linked with those two words, but how? I cannot figure out what this "Project Hybrid" has to do with my life, but I feel like if I continue to explore these images, my answer will soon be revealed.

Twilight. That's what they call me around here. And I guess it fits me since I don't have any memory of my real name and the only thing I know for sure is that that quote is somehow intertwined with me in some way. No one around really knows where I came from or how I ended up here. A few different rumors are passed around but none reliable enough or detailed enough to be of any use to me.

As far as I know, I am all alone here. No family. No one who really knows who I am. According to the whispers, I just randomly appeared here one night. Other rumors I have heard say that the night before I mysteriously showed up, a trail of destruction and mayhem was carved through the city and all of its surroundings.

Although I have no reason to believe it, I feel as though there are others like me, that are connected to this "Project Hybrid," and that could possibly explain what I am and what my purpose is.

A siren goes off. Red lights are flashing. Then an explosion. "What's going on?" Then another explosion, this time closer. "What's happening?" A third explosion, this one directly ahead of me. Then something appeared, a shadowy silhouette emerged from the raging flames caused by the explosion. An ominous feeling swept through the room as the figure drew closer. In a flash, it seemed to manifest itself right in front of my eyes seeming to stare through me as though I didn't exist in its corrupt glare "What are you? Why do you look like...?"

All of a sudden, I jumped up, full of terror as I began to search the room. The room was dark, but I still could not calm myself enough to believe everything was safe. My heartbeat raced, pounding through my chest as I sat in the abandoned apartment, the place I now called my home.

"It was only a nightmare. But why did everything seem so familiar, so real?" Trying to fall back asleep, I laid back staring at the ceiling in hopes of forgetting the face of that malevolent shadow. Just the thought of its horrific gaze and sinister appearance sent a chill that made my skin crawl. But I could not forget that dream. Every time I shut my eyes, even just blinking, led to the image of its face staring through me, and the ominous aura projecting from its presence.

In an attempt to completely remove the image of that dark figure, I decided I would go to the one place where I truly felt safe. The forest on the outskirts of town. At least there, I could be left alone and free of all the worries and memories and just relax. Or at least, that's what I thought...

Dream Turned Into a Nightmare

As I drew closer to my usual place for relaxing, I got the feeling I was being watched. 'But who would be out here? Most people are terrified of this forest, especially coming this deep into an unknown area, and the few who are not scared of the forest fear going anywhere where I spend time.'

Rumors of monstrous creatures living in the forest had been passed down for generations, a way of keep all of the citizens of Pandora within the city limits. To add to the terror, the idea that I was an outsider, something so rarely seen here, made my existence in their walls unbearable. Almost everyone in the city was scared to even be within my presence since, according to the rumors, I was the one who caused all the destruction the night before I was noticed here. Since then, the whole city avoided any contact with me, refusing to talk or even acknowledge my existence when I was around.

All but one person. The one person who was also, supposedly, another mysterious resident of the town and the only person I felt connected to. And the only person I knew was not terrified to go near me. Not only was she not scared to be around me, but she enjoyed it, and did anything she could just to be with me.

Dream. That was her name. And that was exactly who was in my haven. As soon as she noticed me, she stood up and jumped at me in a rush of excitement. She hugged me as if she had not seen me in years and stared up at me, smiling.

She had always been beautiful, ever since I met her. With her long, gorgeous brunette hair that had a glimmer of a golden shine in the sunlight, and her beautiful hazel eyes that looked ever so innocent and kind, along with her lightly tanned, soft skin, she was the ideal girl in every way. At least for me she was, and her personality was what made her even more unique in this nightmare of a world. Kind, loving, carefree, and beautiful, she was definitely one of a kind, a girl worth never losing.

"Twilight! You're here! I knew you would come."

"Yeah, why are you here?" I asked in both a curious and rude manner in hopes of getting her offended enough to leave me here alone. I never liked hurting her, but after my recent nightmare, I needed some alone time.

"I wanted to see you. I had a feeling something was wrong," she said in her cheerful tone, "So is everything okay?"

"Yeah. I'm just fine, as always. I just want to be alone."

"Oh, I'm sorry Twilight. I'll leave." I watched her slowly turn away and walk towards the city. She did it in her disappointed way, unintentionally, the way no one could easily ignore without feeling an ounce of guilt. And she was the only person in Pandora that showed any form of compassion towards me.

"Dream, you can st..." before I could even finish the sentence she came running back to me, giving me one of her well-known hugs that only she could give.

"Thank you, thank you, thank you, Twilight. I promise I won't be a bother." Sitting there, the whole forest felt as though it was still, waiting in anticipation for one of us to break the silence. This forest had a way of being "too quiet", which might have led to some of the rumors of creatures being within its realms. People fear the unknown, and combining the uneasy feelings with the shadows passed over from small woodland animals and windblown branches created the perfect situation for anyone's imagination to erupt wildly.

After a few moments of quiet, Dream broke the silence, "Twilight...? Can I ask you something?"

"Sure. What is it?" I asked, my eyes still shut as I leaned back against a tree.

"Okay, have you ever heard of something called...'Project Hybrid'?" My eyes jolted wide open as I shot straight up, staring directly into her eyes.

"Where did you hear that? What do you know about it?" Without intentionally doing so, I moved in closer to her, which made her both nervous and intimidated, forcing her into backing away from me. She stumbled over a few branches and roots on the ground below, tripping over one of the roots. She fell back against a tree behind her, leaving her trapped up against it with nowhere to go.

"I, I, I don't know..." tears started to fall from her innocent eyes as she turned away to hide her face, "I've been having these dreams lately and every one of them mentions this...'Project Hybrid'. At first I though it was just a coincidence...but not when it happens this often." Staring up at me with tears running down her face, she seemed to be waiting for me to respond to what she said, but I could not respond. I couldn't even move, my body felt as if it were paralyzed, as if all the fear within me was restricting my movements. The same feeling I felt during...that nightmare.

"Tell me this, Dream. Have you ever seen a dark figure in your dreams before?" I started moving in closer while she backed closer to the tree.

"I don't exactly remember, it's all a blur," pausing to compose herself, she calmed down and continued, "I remember sirens going off and seeing a bright flashing red light, but by the time I could move, there was a large section of the walls demolished and fire surrounding the destruction." She paused again to think about everything, then said,

"Now that I think about, there was what I thought was just a shadow at the end of all the destruction that turned its head in my direction and then retreated into the darkness of the night sky. This was all last night."

'Her dream seemed so similar to my own but as if it were viewed from a different perspective. But what does this all mean? What's the connection between the two of us and this Project Hybrid?'

"Dream, were you born here?" A stupid question in most cases since no one living here was born from an outsider, but I had a feeling this would have the answer I both hoped for and feared.

"No, why?" She stared at me puzzled by the question I asked.

I ignored her 'why?' "Where were you born?"

"I don't understand why you're asking all of this. I was born at..." her face lit up with shock as she realized the purpose of my questions. "I, I can't remember where I was born. Why can't I remember where I was born?" she said as she started panicking.

Her eyes, the eyes full of innocence and happiness before, were now full of anger and hatred, focusing directly on me as if it were my fault that she could not remember her past. She focused on me, watching my every movement. The nice, young Dream was no longer here, possessed by this new, more sinister Dream, a completely different, more cruel and destructive persona. She gave off this dark feeling, the same vicious aura as that nightmare-ish shadow.

She let out an ear-piercing shriek, louder than I could ever imagine possible from her. Her shriek wasn't full of terror or fear like most would be, but instead it was fierce and demonic. I didn't know what I should do, or how I should react, but I did know if I didn't do something soon, my nightmare might become a reality.

Her body twitched and I felt a sharp, excruciating pain in my left arm. Attempting to ignore the pain, I watched her movements, and tried to anticipate her next move before it happened again.

Suddenly, I felt this strange, overpowering strength take control of my body. I could no longer move as I stared at Dream, unsure of what would happen when her next strike would take place. Not only did my body change during this new wave of power that erupted through me, but my vision was altered as well.

This time when she twitched again, I was able see her kick coming directly at my right arm. Not only could I see her attempted attack but my body, caught the kick by her ankle, and raised her right leg higher knocking her off balance. With her off balance, I pulled her leg forward, causing her to fall back into a tree behind her.

As she fell back, I could see her eyes change from the sinister glare back to her innocent gaze, then slowly shut. She struggled to stand back on her feet, seeming more exhausted then expected from a simple fall. Her body looked drained of energy as she attempted to look up at me once again, then whispered, "What's going...on? Twilight...What happen...ed?" and collapsed into my arms. Control of my body returned slowly as I stared down at Dream as she lay in my arms, nearly unconscious.

"Dream! Dream! Wake up!" I yelled while trying to keep her conscious. 'This did not make sense; she was fine before. 'What's going on? I can't let her faint here, not out in the wild like this.' I tried every way to wake her without harming her, but with no success.

While trying to keep her awake, the sharp pain in my arm returned. I looked down at my arm and noticed my sleeve tattered, torn and drenched in blood. My eyes blurred and slowly shut as I dropped to my knees, trying to remain conscious myself. Fighting the urge to collapse, I gently began rocking back and forth, losing feeling in my arm, then spreading across my body, going more numb with each passing second. With my last moments of consciousness, I stared at Dream making sure she was okay, whispering,

"Dream...what's...happening...?"...

Clear Slash

Awakening from my unconscious state, I noticed how the surrounding environment had changed over the hours. The bright, radiant glare between the trees from earlier was now a faint glow, shining from the moon and stars hidden in the night sky by the large trees above. The usual noises heard from the small animals throughout the day were now silent. Even the ground, usually warm from the illuminating sun, was causing my body to shiver. But the most dramatic change was that Dream, who had been unconscious in my arms, was gone, nowhere in sight.

I tried gathering up the little energy I could to make my way back to town. Maintaining my balance was the hardest task as of all, as I staggered back through the forest, trying not to stumble with every few steps I took as I leaned against any nearby tree in my path. At the pace I was going through the forest, I was not surprised that it was almost midnight and yet I still had no idea where to go or what I should do. Still terrified after last night's horrific nightmare and today's nightmare-ish encounter, and after the hours of being unconscious, there was no way that I could just go lay down and fall asleep, not that I wanted to even if I could.

Without any other good ideas of what to do at the time, I started searching the city for Dream, in hopes that she could explain what happened earlier. Running out of places to look, my next choice was to check the old abandoned warehouse on the outskirts of town. The warehouse had been abandoned after a mysterious fire tore through a section of the building, and although it was searched and rebuilt, the workers were too terrified to re-enter the factory, forcing it to close.

I searched every inch of the warehouse, trying to use the moonlight streaming through the windows as a source of light. The warehouse had an eerie atmosphere over it, showing little sign of movement within its wall in the years since it closed down. It soon after became the home to spiders, bats, and such creatures that desired dark environments to inhabit.

After searching every corner of the building, I finally found her laying behind a group of boxes in what I guessed she was using as a place to live. She was still asleep and a part of me was terrified to wake her in fear that the other her was still in control, but with no other choice, I started moving in closer to gently wake her.

After lightly shaking her, she awoke and stared up at me, confused and curious.

"Twilight, what are you..." she paused with an expression of terror and shock, "what happened to your arm? Your shirt is all bloody and ripped up! Are you okay?!" It was as if she had no idea what had happened just a few hours prior.

"I'm fine now, Dream. But I have something more important to ask. What happened to you earlier?" I did not want her worrying about my safety and surprisingly my arm was feeling better strangely.

"What do you mean? And how are you fine...your arm is drenched in blood? Let me do something to help." She rose from her "bed" and made her way around the stacks of boxes and crates, disappearing into another room of the warehouse. Where she was and what she was getting were two things that I did not know and yet that was not what was on my mind. I awaited Dream's return just a few inches away from where she was laying, leaned against a large crate as I stared at the door she left through. 'How could I explain what happened this morning to her without her thinking I'm insane? I still can't even believe today's event actually happened and I witnessed it all.'

While distracted by my own thoughts, Dream returned with a bandage wrap and a bottle of rubbing alcohol, and took a seat next to me. She tried to roll up my sleeve to disinfect my cut without touching my skin, unsure of how much was injured or how sensitive the area would be.

"Ok, Twilight, this may sting...a...little? Um, Twilight?" she gently whispered, awaking me from my daze as she stared down at my arm.

"Yeah?"

"Where's the cut? Or at least the scar?"

"What do you mean? Its right he..." It was gone. The cut from that strike early had completely vanished leaving no trace behind. 'But how? I know I was cut earlier, there is nothing that could make me forget the pain that coursed through my body after Dream's assault. So why is there no scar left behind?' 'But even if I somehow did imagine it, make it all up, what torn up my sleeve and covered it in blood? This was not possible. There has to be some explanation. But what?'

"Twilight, who's blood is that..." she asked in a nervous tone. But I could not answer. I didn't have an answer. "Twilight! Tell me!" She backed away in fear of what could have been the cause of my bloodied clothing. Little did she realize, she was the cause. "Twilight!"

"You wouldn't believe me if I told you the truth. No one would." I mumbled as I attempted to respond to her.

"What do you mean? Twilight...did you ki...ki..." she could not finish the sentence, too horrified by the thought of it.

"Kill someone? No, never. You don't have any memory of today?" 'Maybe she wouldn't believe me, but I couldn't lie to her, no matter what,' I thought to myself as I hoped for any answer that would ease the stress of explaining the situation.

"Not really, It's all a blur. I remember being with you in your usual spot in the forest, but after that, I can't really remember. Why?"

"You're not going to believe this but...you did this." Her face filled with shock, confusion and disbelief as I continued my explanation. "Earlier today, you got mad at something I said and attacked me. With a single kick, you sliced a deep gash into my arm, causing what you see here. I don't know how or why the cut has vanished, but I assure you, it was there. You know I wouldn't lie to you Dream." She froze, just staring at me as her eyes filled with tears, just barely able to hold them back. "Drea..."

"No!" she screamed, "You're lying! That's not possible." The wall of tears she was trying so hard to hold back finally broke out. She covered her face and shook her head in disbelief, as if she were trying to forget what I told her.

"Dream...are you okay..." I reached over to touch her, to comfort her, when she slapped away my arm and stared up at me with red, swollen eyes, the tears continued to fall.

"Don't touch me!" She yelled her, face turning completely red with anger and hurt as my words replayed through her head. "Stay away from me!" She ran out the room, vanishing into the darkness of the unlit room.

Standing there, I didn't know what I should have done, if I should follow her or give her time to relax and absorb the information. On the one side, she's the only person who wants to be around me, and yet, I can't handle what happened earlier happening again.

The room I was standing in, filled with darkness and silence, seemed to be getting smaller as time passed, highlighting the exit and the area where she ran off to just moments ago.

Rather than risking any more problems, I decided to give her time alone, time to calm down and reflect on what I told her. I could understand how she was feeling; anyone would feel the same way she did with news similar to what I just gave her. With this time to myself, I could get back to focusing on my true goal for the time being, finding my purpose and discovering what Project Hybrid was.

I left, walked into the darkness of the night in search of some clue for what I needed to find my answers...

Dream's Midnight Encounter

"That can't be true...he has to be lying. How could I have hurt him? I don't even remember seeing him after this morning...or did I? I faintly remember being with him, but...I'd never hurt him. I could never do that to him, he means too much to me. But he wouldn't lie to me?...Right? I mean, he's never lied to me before, but where's the proof? Where's this 'gash' that I supposedly caused in his arm? He has to be lying, there's no other possible explanation for his story. But, I just can't believe that, no matter how much I want to. Twilight wouldn't lie to me. Maybe if I listen to his story more, I can find out the whole truth. Or catch him in his lie."

"Either way, I need to talk to him again." I said while using the wall to help stand back up.   As I took my first step, a sudden pain shot through my leg, making me collapse to the floor in pain as I screamed out in agony. The pain was unbearable, unlike anything I had ever felt before. The dim lighting in this room made it impossible to see what was the source of my agony as I struggled to relieve the pain in any way possible.

'But where is Twilight? By now, he would have come in here to see if I was at least okay. Is he okay? Or maybe he's mad at the way I acted.' I thought to myself as I struggled to ignore the pain and find a way to attract his attention.

"Twilight?" I screamed, hoping to see him come running in, as I tightly gripped my leg over the injured area to ease the pain. 'Still, nothing, complete silence.' "Twilight! I need your help..." I shouted as the intensity of the pain suddenly grew. "Please, Twilight...I need you," I whispered finally realizing he was either gone or didn't care.

Beginning to panic, I feared the worst for why Twilight was not coming to help me. Whether it was because he left me here alone, was offended by my actions before I left him standing there alone in the dark, or even worst, he somehow got hurt out there. I began to

worry as images of all the possible explanations flashed through my head, each one getting

worse by the second. 'What if he got hurt, trapped under crates or anything, because I had

to get offended over his story and stormed out like a little kid. I could never forgive myself

if he somehow got injured because of me.'

Staggering to get back up, I pulled myself up enough to allow me to walk, or at least

make an attempt. I limped to the door to see if Twilight was still around to help me get to

a hospital or something, but the pain from what ever happened to my leg was too

unbearable to continue. I rolled up the leg of my jeans to see what was causing me all this

pain once I got into an area illuminated by the moon's light through a window, and when

I did, I dropped to the floor petrified by the sight.

My leg appeared as if it was shattered inside, with sections darkened with bruises and

scratches that ran across my entire shin. One section even looked like the bone was

crushed under the skin by an incredibly strong force or impact, and yet not a single

fragment of the bone pierced through my skin. Not a drop of blood was exposed from the

shattered section, my skin, although discolored, still remaining intact holding the damage

within. Unable to stare at the sight anymore, I rolled my jeans back down, revealing a

bloodstain that ran across my leg in the same location as the injury.

"But I never bled, how could my jeans be stained? Unless...could this be Twilight's

blood? Could he have been telling the truth?"

I dragged myself across the floor, crawling to the room where I left Twilight still

hoping that he would be there to both forgive and assist me in this time of need. Every

ounce of my strength felt as if it were being drained from my body, leaking from the sealed wound as it dragged against the unfinished cement floor. A movement in the next room caught my attention as the wooden floorboards creaked with each approaching footstep. His outline appeared in the doorway, several feet from where I was, and he simply stared down at me as he remained hidden by the shadows surrounding him.

"Twilight!" I screamed as emotions overwhelmed me, "Why didn't you come help me? Didn't you hear me? Twilight! Answer me!" He just stood there, silent and motionless, watching me ever so closely, making the air feel thick with suspense as I awaited any response from the lifeless figure.

I grabbed a broken fragment of cement and tossed it in his direction, hoping to wake him from the trance he was trapped in.

"Silly little girl," he said in an unfamiliar voice. He finally moved closer, slowly making his way towards me as I watched in horror, unaware of this unknown person's intentions.

"You're not Twilight...who are you?" Nothing, no response from him. I tried to pull myself away and back into another room where I could lock myself in and hide until enough of my strength returned to allow me to escape without this stranger getting a hold of me. But my plan had failed, and by the time I reached the room and tried shutting the door, it was too late. He was standing in the doorway, staring down at me and holding the door open so that I would be unable to shut it even with all of my strength restored. I could hardly see his face as he remained in the shadows around, avoiding any light from shining upon his person. He reached down and grabbed my shattered bone, squeezing it within his tight grip as I let out a shriek of misery and anguish.

Using my unharmed leg, I kicked him away and stumble up to a position where I could attempt to run. Ignoring the pain from my injury, I ran into the darkness of the next room, a section where I knew I would be completely hidden from anyone's sight.

"You couldn't escape even if you wanted to, my dear. Yet you have no reason to fear, I'm not here to harm you," He said as he stared into the abyss, scanning for my location.

"You're lying." I whispered accidently, hoping he did not hear me enough to find where I was hiding. He stared directly at me, as if he could see me perfectly fine, but did not make any attempt to move closer.

"Oh yeah? Check your 'injury'." He replied with a sense of sarcasm in his voice. I rolled up my jeans ready to see a crushed, shattered bone again but this time, I was wrong. 'My leg is looks fine, good as new, but how?'

"What...what did you do?" I whispered as I walked out from the darkness.

"Come with me young Dream, and all will be explained." he said while turning his back to me and walking towards the warehouse exit.

"Wait," I yelled as he almost left the room, "I'll come with you...but first, who are you?"

He turned around to face me as he answered my question, "Ah, where are my manners? They call me...Midnight."...

The Nightmare Returns

As time passed by, more questions continued to arise, and yet no answers had been unveiled. 'Who am I? What is my purpose? Am I alone? Why am I here? And the most important question as of right now, what is Project Hybrid?'

I felt as though the answers to all of my questions would be answered if I could just find the origin of this mysterious project. 'But where do I start? Do I leave here and abandon my "home" in search of my answers or do I stay here in hopes of a clue coming to me instead?'

'As of right now, it would be too late to leave if I wanted to make it through the forest without risking getting lost or mauled by any nocturnal animals. For now, I had to wait until at least sunrise to make my way out of here.'

'That's it, I'm leaving at dawn. For now, I need to rest if I'm going to make it out without collapsing from exhaustion.' I shut my eyes and daydreamed of what had happened earlier today with Dream. 'I hope she's okay...'

A familiar sound began to replay over and over in the distance, almost like a fire alarm...or a siren. Recognizing the situation, I turned, facing the walls directly behind me. "Is this really happening again?" Then the three explosions erupted, shattering the structure directly ahead of me, once again igniting the frames surrounding creating a massive flame that spread across the debris. Then it appeared, the nightmare-ish figure that remained engraved in the back my head every moment of the day. This time, I could see it more clearly though, with what looked like two wings sprouting from its back, one like that of an eagle and one similar to a bat. Rather than seeming like an enormous, demonic figure, it seems smaller, almost the size of an average person. And yet, its eyes remained horrifying and entrancing, sending a chill down my spine.

But this time things seemed to be different, rather than giving off the same ominous feeling like last time, it seemed more familiar, as if somehow it was connected to me. It vanished into the darkness of the night sky in a flash of light but instead of the dream ending at this point as it did last night, it continued as I watched the colossal building crumble into the enraged flames. Then I realized why the dream had not ended. There was more to the mystery as the dream continued to play through my mind.

Another figure appeared from the wreckage, this one smaller than the last but it still gave off a destructive aura, different from the last but just as dangerous, as it disappeared in a blur. A third emerged, this one as terror-inducing as the first nightmare. It stared up into the night sky, the air feeling thick and motionless in its presence. The creature raised its head and stared in my direction with eyes that spiraled around the center, as if it could see me when the others could not. After a few seconds, it let out a vicious howl, raised its arm to the sky and vanished as the others did.

My body jolted into an upright position as I put my arms up in a defensive position to protect myself instinctually. "Another dream..." I told myself as I tried to relax again. "But this one at least gave me more information. To what, I still don't know but I do know that that shadow isn't alone. But how can I use this information to help find my answers? Maybe, if I can find the building that was demolished in the destruction, that'll give me a clue. Or maybe, it's my job to hunt down those three...monsters."

I rose and stared up at the still moonlit sky as I realized that hardly any time has passed. "Maybe Dream had the same nightmare as I just did. I need to find her and talk to her. I don't care if the other Dream shows up, I need answers."

I set out to the warehouse I last saw Dream at in hopes that she was still there to question...

The Path to Midnight

I rushed over to Dream's warehouse, hoping that she was still there so I could try explaining myself to her once more in a more peaceful manner than the past two attempts. Forcing my way through the door, I heard the screech of rusted hinges collapsing under the pressure as the door came crashing down. Searching frantically for her, I worried leaving her there alone in the way she was early was a bad idea. With fewer and fewer places to check, I searched every dark corner in the warehouse.

"Dream! Dream! Where are you?" I yelled with each passing second that she remained hidden from my sight. Reaching the point where most people would give up the search, I panicked as my thoughts of something happening to her increased with each area I searched with no success. Running out of options, I made my way back to the main entrance; the collapsed door lay in the open path illuminated by the night sky.

Standing in the doorway was a dark figure, staring at me yet almost in a daze, as if it was under an extreme form of hypnosis. "Dream? Is that you?" It said nothing. I moved in closer, trying to see if it was Dream as the darkness around it hid its features from my vision. "Dream?" With each step, its outline became more defined, revealing the body shape of the young girl I searched for. The clothing she was wearing verified my observation as the light shined on the entranced Dream. 'What's wrong with her? Why isn't she moving or acknowledging me?'

I grabbed her arm and shook her in an attempt of snapping her out of whatever daze she was in, and yet she still stood there, under the control of another, no longer herself. "Dream? It's me, Twilight." I kept repeating as I shook her, trying to wake her from this trance. Finally, she acknowledged my existence as she looked up at me with a cold, lifeless stare. "Are you okay?"

"Twilight. Come with me, Twilight. I have someone you have to meet." She said in a zombified tone.

"Who? And what's wrong with you? Dream?"

"Follow me and I'll show you."

"Wait!" I yelled as she turned and walked away, entering the darkness of the forest. "Dream, stop! Tell me what's going on." Nothing I said had an effect on her; she just kept walking, almost disappearing in the shadows from the tree. With no other choice, I decided I needed to follow her. I ran into the forest after her, trying to catching up with her as she continued through the forest. With each step I took, visions of those three nightmarish characters replayed.

Finally catching up with Dream, I pulled at her arm, spinning her around to face my direction as I questioned her. "Dream, have you had any more nightmares lately?" "All your questions will be answered soon enough." She replied in that zombified tone once again.

"Answer me, Dream. Who are you taking me to see?"

"You'll know when midnight arrives..."

"Midnight, that was hours ago. Why are we here? Are you expecting me to wait until midnight once again for whomever you're taking me to see?" Rather than replying to any more of my questions, she turned away and continued her path through the trees. Without any other choice, I decided I would simply follow her so that "All my questions can be answered". Recognizing the path we are taking, I began to wonder why we are going there.

"Here we are, Twilight." she said as she stopped, staring into the dark bushes ahead.
"Stay here. He'll be here soon."

"Wait, where are you going? Who are you talking about?" Ignoring all of my
questions once more, she walked off into the darkness ahead.

I remained where she asked me to wait, awaiting the person Dream wanted me to
speak with. 'Who could this be that Dream lured me out into the forest to speak with
rather than back in Pandora? At least I can relax here while I wait in my usual spot.' I took
a seat on the ground and leaned against a nearby tree, searching around to see if anyone, or
thing, was in the area. Nothing seemed to be around me as I scanned the forest floor for
any signs of movement. The area seemed secure, until a leaf dropped from above,
reminding me to check the trees as well. I stared up into the shadows of the trees, unable
to see much but the faint glow of green from light shining through the healthy leaves. But
a hint of gray, and a darkened area in the trees caught my eyes. I focused my attention on
the figure in the trees, and watched as the reflection from glasses over its eyes shined in the
sky…

A Test of Time

As I focused on the figure in the tree above, another movement caught my attention as it flashed passed the corner of my eye, dashing from limb to limb overhead. Then another jolt of movement scrambled through the nearby bushes. More movements seemed to be appearing around me with each passing minute, all concealed by the darkness projected across the forest. A chill of terror flowed through my veins as I attempted to track the flow of motion that was swarming around me.

It was as if everything in the forest had become riled up by an unknown force, not as a distraction, but fleeing in terror. Animals scurried through the forest, struggling to get away from the cause of their fear.

Not only were the movements distracting my attention, but the sounds created by all of the hidden motions were causing my sense to go insane as I tried to track it all while still watching the figure above. One shadow distracted me just enough to lose my focus on whoever was in the tree. Before I could look back up again, it had vanished to an unknown location. Small branches snapping, leaves crunching, limbs shaking, wolves howling, bats and birds screeching, all synchronized to cause my senses to go wild in an attempt to scout out what it was that was causing all of this, and where the original figure had disappeared to.

"Make it stop!" I screamed as I held my head in hopes of drowning out some of the noises, but to little avail. The sounds pierced through my skull, tearing my sanity apart as the sounds of the forest grew louder. I backed away, shaking my head as my hands began to tremble from the pain coursing through my skull. "Stop this…Now!"

Then, within the second, it all stopped. All the movements just ceased and all the noises of the forest went silent as if it never happened. Everything was still, lifeless, petrified without a sound to justify what was happening.

It was as though everything was frozen in time, without a motion for miles to justify the cause for the sudden halt. The silence became more unbearable than the rapid movements and noises that were driving me insane just moments ago. "But how could it all stop like that?" I mumbled to myself, and yet even that could not be heard. The entire area was turned into a vacuum; no sounds could be heard for miles, making it impossible to track anything using any sense but sight.

As I searched the surrounding area for my target, an eerie feeling passed over me, as I realized everything around me was literally frozen in time. A lone wolf suspended in mid-air, a single owl staring down at me with wings extended to take off, were both motionless in their captured positions.

A movement in the bushes broke through the time barrier and emerged from its cover, yet remained shrouded by the shadows surrounding it. The enshrouded visitor gave off the same dark aura as the creatures from my nightmares and Dream, and yet seemed more in control of itself and its surroundings. Concealed in a veil of darkness, I could not see who, or what, it was that watched me with an uninterrupted stare.

Without any signs of change, time within the forest continued as it was moments ago, yet the intensity of sounds and motions dulled. The lifeless owl flew off into the night and the petrified wolf continued its path through the forest. The sounds of the forest flowed through the air, allowing for a sense of relief as my surroundings returned to normal. I let out a sigh, my worries seeming to be over, for the moment…

The Uncontrolled Face-Off

The moment of happiness was short-lived as I realized the reason it all began was standing directly ahead of me, watching my every movement. "Twilight," the figure began with in a well-mannered tone as he approached, "it's been so long, my old friend. What's wrong? You look as though you have no idea who I am?..." He began to laugh in a villainous, almost maniacal manner as he continued, "Oh that's right. You don't remember me. You can't. None of you can. One of the tragic downfalls of the unfinished 'Project Hybrid'."

"Who are you? What do you know about Project Hybrid? Tell me!" I shouted as I moved in closer towards him. I felt the anger and confusion swelling within me as it tried to take control of my actions. I grabbed his jacket and forced him against a tree, pinning him in place as I continued, "How do you know me? Answer me!" He began to chuckle, as though he knew this would happen, and it grew louder, into that laugh yet again.

"Still as naive as ever. And foolish."

"Wha..." Before I could even finish my sentence, he ran his fist into my chest, knocking the air out of me and forcing my grip loose. As I tried to recover, he wrapped his hand around my throat, reversed our positions, and slammed my back against the tree while holding my body in the air with one arm.

"Listen before you act, Twilight, it's an easy way not to make new enemies."

"O...k...ay" I muttered as I struggled for air through his grip.

"Good." He released my throat from his grip, allowing my body to drop to the floor as I gasped for air and tried to regain my energy from his last impact. I could not gather the strength to stand, as I knelt on the floor bent over in pain and shock. I silently waited for him to continue what he was saying before as I sat back against the tree.

"Now since you asked, I'll tell you my name, or at least what I am known as. I'm known as Midnight and I am the same as you."

Using the little strength I could gather up to stand back up to face him evenly, I asked, "What do you mean...we're the same?"

"Exactly what I said. You, me, Dream, we're all the same."

"Dream?" I whispered, "What did you do to Dream?"

"Just explained the truth to her," he said with a cynical smile. Rage began to swarm within me as the thoughts of this 'new' Dream replacing the young, carefree Dream pierced even the deepest depths of my mind. As my rage grew, a feeling unknown to me, a feeling of both pure and corrupt mien, awakened within me. With each passing second, I lost control to this new power as it swelled within me.

"And so the dark and light have arrived..." he stated in a proud manner continuing with that insulting laugh yet again. The laugh that drove my sanity to its limits as I attempted to bottle up the force within that seemed to be winning the war for control of my body. As the laugh pulled me closer to insanity, command of my movements was pulled away at the same rate.

Without manipulation from my own mind, my arm slowly clenched its fist in preparation for what was soon to come. My body turned from its original position facing Midnight into a sideways stance with my head staring down at the shadows produced by the moonlit trees above. A single leaf fell slowly, rocking back and forth in the air as it made its way to the ground. As it touched down, the long awaited moment occurred as I spun my body forward, swinging my arm until my tightly clenched fist made contact with his open jaw, silencing his laugh. His body crashed down onto the floor with such incredible force; it bounced and rolled across the floor, smashing into a tree.

I walked over to the now silent, motionless body and picked him up by his throat, pinning him against the scarred tree as I stared at him, awaiting his next move. He began to clap, as he slowly raised his head until he was staring me directly in the eyes, blood dripping from his lips as he attempted to smile. His eyes were different, completely inhuman and unlike any I had seen before; the green eyes that he once had were white with three sets of black rings surrounding a black pupil. I tightened my grip, attempting to remove the smile from his blood-stained lips yet he continued to stare, the smile spreading across his face.

"Ahhh, so you even have the eyes? Very nice." He murmured as the blood dripping from his mouth ceased. "So you're already this far, I'm impressed."

'How is this possible? How did he survive that unharmed? And how can I do all of this when earlier he could easily counter my attack?' I thought to myself as he continued to clap.

"Well done, Twilight. I see the darkness is as strong as ever...," he said as he laughed and clapped, but within a moment his tone switched over to a more serious, intimidating manner, "Now, let's test the light!"

His body jolted as he grabbed the arm that was suspending his body off the ground, lifted his legs to my chest level and pushed away, forcing loose my grip and freeing himself. As I stumbled back and tried to regain my balance, he was into his next attack. He ran at me, as though he was charging an attack with his arm behind him while the rest of his upper body remained bent low. As I attempted to brace myself for the impact, I realized it was futile; I was not in control and the unknown force had a plan of its own.

Instead of getting into a defensive position or attempting to retreat, my body mimicked his movements, charging forward in the same stance as he, even mimicking as he swung his 'charged' attack. Both fists collided with a great intensity, and for a second, the impact caused a bright white light to emit between the collision that soon faded as some strange force threw us back, causing us both to crash into surrounding trees. Midnight's impact tore throw the trunk of the tree he originally collided into, causing him to smash against another behind that. 'No one could survive that...' I thought to myself as I watched his seemingly lifeless body.

His body remained motionless as it lie on the ground under the remains of the collapsed tree, his clothes bloody and torn from the impact. I moved in closer just to confirm my suspicions when a movement nearby caught my attention. I scanned the area, searching through the darkness for the source when a familiar sound broke the silence. Clapping. Midnight walked out from the shadows, revealing himself as I focused on his location.

"How?" I yelled as I slowly regained control.

"You did well, Twilight. No wonder they thought so highly of you. Looks like destiny is unfolding exactly as planned." He said as he smiled at me, "You may be more of a use to me after all. Until we meet again..." That was the last thing he said as he vanished into thin air, leaving no trace behind. This time he looked different though, his eyes were green instead of the previous look and his hair was a different shade, more of a dark gray than the silver it had just been.

"Tw...i...light," a voice whispered from behind. I recognized the voice as I instinctively stuck out my arms, catching her before she hit the ground. It was Dream, and she seemed to be back to normal finally. And so did I surprisingly. 'What was all that? How could I do all of that damage, and how could he handle all of it and return unharmed? There are still many questions that remain unanswered, but this Midnight seems to know.'

'For now, my priority is Dream. Although she is back to normal, she needs to rest.' I carried her over to a nearby tree and held her close as she gently fell into her own dream world. As I sat and watched her, I felt myself slowly falling asleep as well...

A Ghostly Encounter

"Twilight!" The sound echoed through my head.

"Twilight!" I opened my eyes, seeing blurry silhouette glaring down at me, yet I couldn't tell who, or what, it was. A few blinks while rubbing my eyes quickly cleared everything up. I was no longer in the forest where Dream and I had fallen asleep. I was in some kind of abandoned warehouse judging by the appearance of the room, or at least the little I could see that was not shrouded by the shadows of the windowless room. As I grew more aware of the situation, I noticed Dream was gone as well, no longer in my arms or anywhere to be found.

"Maybe this is another nightmare." I said to myself, using the wall behind me to stand up so I could explore more of the facility. As I scanned the room for any movements, an eerie feeling I was being watched came over me. I could sense some kind of presence nearby, more than one, in the room watching my every move. A movement broke the stillness of the room, attracting my attention to it as I tracked its movements throughout the room. It moved closer with each passing second as I gained the feeling whatever it was moving towards me was not human.

Another presence caught my attention as a glimpse of light appeared in the corner of my eye then vanished as quickly as it appeared. Whatever caused that light was approaching me as I backed away towards the wall, leaving myself trapped and cornered. "This has to be an illusion," I said in a panicked tone as I awaited the two shadows to reveal themselves, "it can't be real."

"In a way, you are correct Twilight. We are, in a way, illusions." one said in a calm, relaxing way, easing my nerves as it approached.

"But we do exist, and you have had a few "encounters' with us before," remarked the other in a more sinister manner.

The more kind spirit moved closer, revealing itself to be covered in a white cloak that covered all parts of its body, along with a hood that cast a shadow over its face, its identity unknown. It had white with blue-ish highlighted, wings that were similar to those of an eagle. "Think back to the time with Dream, and more recently..."

"Midnight!" the more demonic creature interrupted with as he let out a growl that echoed throughout the room. The creature emerged from the darkness surrounding, exposing its true figure as it grew closer. It seemed to be wearing a pair of dark jeans and an obsidian hoodie, also concealing its face under a hood. Its body was deformed, fiendish, with an animal-like posture. It too had wings, but instead they were black with sanguine tips and streaks running through them, looking similar to those of a bat. As it approached, I noticed it razor-like claws extending from each fingertip and jagged fangs that looked like the teeth of a wolf. The most terrifying part of all was its eyes, pure black and infernal, striking terror into me as it glared at me, leaving my body feeling numb.

"We must go now." The creature said in its horrific tone.

"We'll have to continue this another time...soon." the spirit added.

"How will I find you?"

"We're always with you, Twilight."

"And if you must continue this so soon, we shall come again tonight to finish what must be said."

"But..." I tried to ask another question, but they vanished, one in a flash on light and the other shrouded by the surrounding darkness. With that, my senses of the two

apparitions were gone...

The Next Step

"Twilight..." I heard being whispered overhead.

"Twilight...wake up" The familiar voice whispered in a gentle way while lightly nudging my body. I felt around, my eyes still shut, feeling roots and plants that spread across the entire floor, reminding me that I was still leaned against a tree in the middle of the forest. After a few seconds, I opened my eyes to see who was trying to wake me, revealing Dream silhouette standing over me, half covering the sunlight shining directly on me.

"Oh, I'm sorry Twilight," she said as she moved over, completely blocking the sun from shining in my eyes, allowing me to see clearly and adjust my eyes. "Better now," she said with a big smile spread across her face.

"What time is it?" I murmured while trying to sit up straight.

"I'm not really sure. It looks like it's pretty early still."

"Okay." 'The earlier, the better,' I thought to myself as I remembered the two spirits that appeared last night. "So you look like you're back to normal again."

"What do you mean?"

"Eh, nothing. I'm just glad everything is back to normal for now and yesterday is finally over."

"Okay?" she said with a puzzled look on her face. "Are you okay?"

"Yeah, just had a nightmare is all." I couldn't explain what happened last night, even I had no clue what went on last night so how could I explain it to her. "Do you remember a guy named Midnight?"

"I know that name. I met him last night I think." she paused to think, "Yeah, I did because I remember my leg was hurt and he somehow healed it. That reminds me, where did you go last night, I needed you."

"I had to do some thinking and I thought you wanted to be left alone. What do you mean your leg was hurt and he healed it?"

"I don't know. Like when I left the room, my leg appeared to be shattered and yet he grabbed my leg and it was perfectly fine when he let go."

"He grabbed you?" A little anger grew inside me as I wondered if he harmed her in anyway.

"Yeah, why? Jealous?" She said in a perky way while she laughed at the thought.

"No..." Inside I was a little jealous but more bothered by the fact that a stranger grabbed her while I was gone. "Do you remember anything else?"

"Not really. He mentioned answering all of my questions but after that it's all blank up until I saw you last night in the forest the few seconds before I fainted."

"Do you know how to get in touch with him or anything?"

"No. I'm sorry Twilight, I don't remember anything from last night."

"Okay. It's fine. You've at least given me some information."

"You know him?"

"Not only do I know him. I fought him last night." She gasped, an expression on shock on her face as I said those words.

"Are you okay?"

"Yeah, it was strange though. I wasn't in control of my movements and it wasn't a normal fight. It was as if it were something supernatural, a battle between monsters rather than people." I took a deep breath and continued, "not only that, but it seemed as though instead of fighting, he was just testing my strength. He knew about both of us, and Project

Hybrid. He wasn't a normal person, and we need to find him if we have any hopes of

finding any explanation for us." I gave her a few seconds to absorb all that I had just said,

realizing in most cases a person hearing a story like this would find me psychotic.

"Surprisingly, I believe you Twilight. You wouldn't lie to me and you seem too

serious to be making this up. Plus it does sound like it connects with what you told me

before." I let out a sigh of relief, knowing that she was on my side and that nothing bad

would happen if I continue my explanation.

"Oh, and do my eyes look any different?"

"No, should they?"

"I don't know. When I was fighting Midnight last night, he said 'You even have the

eyes' or something like that."

"Well they look normal to me."

"We have to find him again."

"But why? He fought you last night, and I don't want you getting hurt this time."

"I know but he knows the answers we need." I stared up at the sky considering other

choices. "Or...we could try to find this abandoned factory or laboratory or whatever it was

that I saw in my nightmare last night. That might hold the clues to some answers we

desire."

"So let's go there. Anywhere that won't get you hurt." She said while looking away,

trying to hide her emotions.

"Well it's not in the city. We'll have to start looking somewhere new."

"Okay...so let's get ready."

"Let's get going right now..." I said while using the tree to keep my balance as I stood up.

"Wait." She whispered gently.

"For what?"

"Well we need to get changed...especially you, your clothes are all torn up." I looked down at my clothes, noticing my shirt was torn up from the two fights and my jeans were all scuffed and scratched.

"Well I guess we can go do that then go. Where are we going to get clothes?"

"At the warehouse you found me at yesterday, there are crates full of clothes nobody wants in there."

"Okay let's go then."

Back at the warehouse, she jumped and skipped around in excitement as she picked out an outfit to wear.

"What should I wear?" She kept mumbling as she ran from crate to crate.

"Anything comfortable that won't slow you down." I said in hopes of getting her to speed up.

"Well you pick out your stuff and by the time you do that and get changed, I'll be ready."

"Okay." I walked up to a large crate that had a label on it smudged and torn from years of being unused. Searching inside, I picked up a white sleeveless shirt, black jeans, and a long hooded overcoat.

I brought all of the clothes I picked out into another room nearby where I changed into the new outfit. All of it fit well at first, but when I lifted my arms in the overcoat, the sleeves tore from being overstretched, leaving holes around the top of both sleeves. I grabbed each sleeve and tore them off to see how the coat would look without them. Staring in the mirror, I decided to leave my outfit the way it is. The now sleeveless black overcoat fit perfectly with the look I was going for as I checked in the mirror.

"Are you ready Dream?" I said as I walked out fixing my coat.

"Yes, just give me one sec." She yelled from another room. I sat down on an unopened crate awaiting her arrival as I stared at my new outfit. A pure white, sleeveless shirt, a pair of jet black jeans, and a torn sleeveless, onyx overcoat with layers near the bottom that had blood red tips on each edge. 'This outfit is exactly the way I would want it to be' I thought to myself.

"So what do you think?" Dream said as she walked out from the darkness. She looked amazing, wearing a pair of black leggings, with a blue and green skirt over it and a white blouse on top. I couldn't even describe how beautiful she looked and she seemed to notice as she began to blush and giggle. She walked up to me, "Wow, you look great. I like that outfit." she said smiling. "But one thing is missing."

"What's that?"

"This..." she pulled out a necklace with a black metal chain that had a crystal, half-black and half-white hanging on the end. She reached around my neck, put it on for me, and leaned back saying, "Perfect. Count it as a good luck charm from me." Still as close as she was before, she leaned forward and kissed my cheek with her soft, smooth lips gently, and whispered in my ear, "Thanks for protecting me and staying with me all night."

Now I was the one smiling as she pulled my hand and said, "Well let's get going before it gets too late to leave."

We walked out and made our way back through the forest...

A Third Joins the Search

As we made our way through the forest, we both remained silent, unaware of what to say to each other, or where we were even going. Once we reached my haven, Dream stopped and turned, as though she had something on her mind. "Twilight." She said in a low tone, while looking down at the ground.

"Yes, Dream?"

"What if we do all this searching and we still don't find an answer to our past..." She paused to find a way to phrase what she wanted to say next, "...or worse. What if you get hurt from this search? I..."

"That won't happen, Dream. Maybe we won't solve all of our questions with this, but if not, we'll keep searching until we do. And I won't get hurt for two reasons. One is that I have this power within me that refuses to let anything happen to me..." She looked up at me waiting for the second reason. "And the second reason, I have my good luck charm," I said as I held up the necklace she gave me and smiled.

Her eyes lit up with joy when I said that and she tackled me with a hug full of emotions. "Promise me, you'll never let anything bad happen to you no matter what." Tears ran down her face as she awaited my response.

"I promise. And same goes for you, promise you won't let anything happen and you'll stay safe always."

"I promise. As long as I have you, nothing can happen to me, right?" she said with a smile on her face. She wiped away her tears, and turned to face the unexplored section of the forest.

"From here on out, we have to travel by instinct and using any information from our visions that we can. And be careful, we don't know what is out there lurking in the shadows."

"But I do..." a voice from above said.

"It can't be..." I slowly turned back and looked up at the trees surrounding us, noticing a figure sitting up high on a limb staring down at us. It dropped down like a brick, only to land on its feet in the shadows cast from above, but the voice was too familiar to be unaware of whom it is. "Midnight."

"So you recognized me that quickly? Nice memory."

"Of course. I remember it all. What are you doing here?"

"Relax." He walked towards us, revealing light gray suit pants and a blue dress shirt covered by a light gray jacket. He looked like an entrepreneur or something within that general area but his face still remained disguised by the shadows above. "I'm not here to fight, but instead to help."

"How?"

"By joining you in your search and assisting you through the forest."

"What's in it for you?"

"I've got my reasons, and my own questions to solve. And since we're all 'Hybrids', I think joining you two would be best to help prepare you."

"Prepare us for what?" Dream asked from behind me, peaking her head around in curiosity.

"I'll explain on the way, now am I in or not?"

I waited a few seconds to respond, running each possible outcome through my head to assure my choice was the correct one. "You're in. Now start explaining."

"Well let's walk and talk." He stepped out of the shadows, revealing his sinister smile as he fixed his silver-rimmed glasses raising them back to eye level, hiding his eyes with the glare from the sun reflected off his glasses.

"Well let's get moving, night is approaching." 'Is trusting him worth the risk?' I thought to myself as we set out again into the unknown...

A New Mystery Revealed

The forest seemed darker the more we traveled into the unexplored areas, as if something evil resided among the mass of trees surrounding. I had to make sure I kept my guard up twice as much, to both defend myself and protect Dream as I promised I would.

"Well, Midnight, start explaining." I said while searching our surroundings for any potential threats. "Tell us what you know about us and Project Hybrid."

"Ah, where to start?" He said with a smile as he waited for me or Dream to say anything. "We are a trio destined to meet and complete the tasks of the ones who created us."

"Created?" Dream mumbled under her breath.

"Yes, created. We were part of an experiment in which a group of geneticists gathered to create the perfect living weapons, a hybrid of both life and weaponry if you will. They even devised that rather than have one uncontrollable weapon, they would split it into three separate individual weapons, making a fail-safe in case one of the three loses control. Or at least that's what they thought would happen."

"What do you mean that's what they thought would happen?" I asked as I became drawn into this story more and more.

"Well, I was the first of the three part experiment known as Project Hybrid. Once I was a success, they began creating you, Twilight, and shortly after Dream as well. My memory of all of this remains solely due to timing, while you two were not complete at the time. Dream was just nearing the end steps of the process, and you were for some reason declared a failed experiment. And yet they never gave up on you, mentioning how they had high hopes for you and needed you to stay. Each of us were given a supernatural element to control in which once we were together, nothing could harm us. I was given

the ability to control and warp time and space, as you may or may not have discovered in

our earlier encounter. Dream was given the ability to create vast and complex illusions,

well enough that even you and I can't tell the difference between reality and her illusions,

the ultimate defense for any situation that we could not handle directly. And you, you

possess the ability to control both darkness and light, which can be used as either a form of

offense or defense." He paused for a second to see if we had any questions or if we were lost

then continued, "Little did they expect that they're precious Twilight would lead to the

end of the project in an abrupt and explosive manner." He smiled when he said that, as if

he just told the punch line to a joke we couldn't understand.

"What do you mean?" Both Dream and I asked simultaneously without intention.

"Well, do you recall having dreams of a building on fire and three silhouettes

emerging then vanishing without an explanation?"

"Yes..."

"Well that explosion and first figure, that was you Twilight. And the next to emerge

was Dream, and finally I escaped into the night."

"Impossible!" I shouted, stopping in my tracks with my focus directly on Midnight.

"Actually, it's very possible and did happen. As they were conducting another test on

you in hopes of unlocking some of your true potential, something went wrong and you

awakened in a fit of rage, using your elements to destroy the lab, freeing Dream and I, and

escaping into the forest where I'm guessing both you and Dream ended up in that town

back there."

"So all of those rumors...about the destruction through the forest..."

"Yes. They are true, and caused by you." My mind was going wild, thoughts of all of the visions I had as I realized it was all true. "It's actually ironic that you and Dream met up and became such good friends before I arrived."

Dream noticed I was in shock and began asking her own questions. "But how do you remember all of this?"

"As I said, it was a matter of timing. I was complete before the incident so I hardly lost anything, I kept most of my memories and have most control over my powers. Unlucky for you, you and Twilight never completed the steps to reaching complete hybridization so your memories, along with your powers, are still locked deep within you. Yet they still come out through your dreams, and it seems through your anger as well."

"How do we gain control of our powers then?"

"That, I can't help with. My powers were unlocked through the experiment, but yours both weren't awakened thoroughly so you both must find the way to unlock them, and soon."

I snapped out of my trance to hear that part. "Why soon?"

"Because the reason we were created is growing near."

"What is that?"

"To find and exterminate an enemy's creations somehow. But that information even I do not know. We were supposed to be briefed of our mission once both of you reached hybridization, but that never happened."

"Well how can we find out?"

"Possibly by going to the remains of the old laboratory and finding a file containing the information we require. Hopefully it still remains there."

"And if it doesn't?"

"Then we won't know who to find until they find us." We all stayed silent after that as we awaited the other to begin the conversation again.

I broke the silence, "So you're taking us to the laboratory right now?"

"Yes. And be prepared, I don't know what we will encounter once we get closer."

I looked over at Dream, who was now the silent one and moved closer to help comfort her. "Dream, remember my promise? It's still in effect." I said with a smile as I wrapped my arm around her, holding her close and tight. "Midnight, have you ever seen two spirits? One angelic and one demonic?"

"No, why? Have you?"

"Yes, and I'm supposed to see them again to find answers to my questions."

"Well find out about our enemy, or enemies, if that's possible."

"Will do."

"And so the destined trio is once again reunited." He said with a smirk of his face.

We stayed silent for the rest of the travel to through part of the forest as I held Dream to keep her calm and keep myself feeling human rather than like a monster. 'Maybe that's what Dream is thinking too'...

The Trials Begin

The forest only seemed to get darker with each passing second even though the sun was still high in the sky, and soon even that was clouded by the void of darkness. Vision became limited and to prevent any accidents, I held Dream close with her behind me so that she would not walk into anything or get lost in the unknown.

"Twilight...I'm scared." Dream whispered from behind.

"Well keep close to me. I'll keep you safe." Midnight seemed unaffected by the lack of vision and continued to lead the way through the darkness as if it were light out. "Hey Midnight, how do you know where you're going?"

"I've traveled this path many times before in attempt of finding the laboratory and uncovering the secret unknown to even me but have failed each time."

"How did you fail?"

"The secrecy of Project Hybrid was far more important than you realize. In order to protect the facility and everything within it, a set of three trials were set in which only the trio could pass through without harm. Knowing that I am part of that trio, I thought that I could get through on my own, but soon learned that the trio must be complete before entrance may be granted."

"What are the trials?"

"The first is this veil of shadows in which we are trapped in now. This trial is meant to test my ability of controlling space and sensing my surrounding. You too could travel through hear with ease if you had awakened your dominance over light but without that, I must lead the way."

"What's the next trial?" Dream mumbled as she clenched onto my arm.

"The next is for you, Dream. It is an area created by an illusion that seems rather large although the actual length is short in distance. You must use your powers to bring us to reality so that we can pass through without any risks. I spent what felt like days trapped in this illusion, unaware of how powerful it was and how little control my ability possessed over it."

"But..." She mumbled under her breathe, "I haven't awakened, or whatever you call it, my powers either."

"Yours can be unlocked through your emotions, similar to Twilight, but you will lose control over your body for the time being, and at that time, we must take advantage of your hybrid form and travel through as quickly as possible."

"No." I said with a hint of anger in my voice. "We'll find another way that won't cause harm to Dream in anyway."

"There is no other way..." As Midnight finished that sentence, a ferocious growl echoed from within the darkness surrounding us.

"What was that?" Dream screamed as she hugged me from behind, burying her face into my back to avoid seeing anything.

"I...don't know."

"What do you mean? How do you not know? You said you've been here many times." I shouted as the hint of anger grew to a more noticeable degree.

"I've never heard that before."

A shadow flashed between the trees, moving at speeds I couldn't track. "I just saw it. It's big."

"What does it look like?" Midnight asked with terror in his voice.

"I can't tell. It's moving too fast."

"Not anymore." The creature stopped high up among the limbs above and let out a roar as a warning. It dropped down launching a cloud of dirt and debris into the air as it hit the ground and stayed bent low, ready to attack.

"Don't move." I whispered to Midnight as we both stayed motionless.

"I can handle this." He raised his hand with his palm towards the creature as if he were preparing an attack. "Freeze," He whispered while throwing his arm down, forcing everything around us to cease and ending the hiss it was letting out towards us. "Let's go." He looked back and motioned for us to continue through the forest onto the next trial when a movement caught my eye.

"Look out!" I dove at him, knocking him onto the ground just in time to avoid the creature's sneak attack. It charged at us, snarling and growling, and pounced at Midnight in the moment of distraction where he thought it was frozen. I watched as its large, wolf-like body tore past us with incredible speed before landing and retreating into the darkness that enveloped us.

"What was that?" Midnight shouted in both anger and fear. "And how did it escape my technique?"

"It looked like some kind of wolf-like creature with human characteristics. It definitely was nothing created by nature alone. It must guard this section of the trial from any who make it this far." Midnight just stood there in a trance as he tried to comprehend what was happening. "Looks like this trial has more within it then even you know. Let's keep moving before it returns."

"We should enter the next trial shortly if we continue this path undisturbed."

Midnight said once the shock of the previous incident was relieved. "Dream, we need you for this trial or else we will be trapped in the illusion without a possibility of getting through."

"Okay..." She said as she stared ahead, keeping look out for any more unwanted visitors.

A branch to the right of us snapped and before I had a chance to comprehend what was going on, I saw the creature dash out from the bushes at us baring claws that tore through the air as it launched its body directly at me. With little time to think or react, my body took control the same way it did while fighting Midnight and bent back just far enough that it narrowly missed its target. Simultaneously, I raised both arms above my head and locked my fingers together, and when the creature was half way past, I used the strength of my combined fists to send it crashed to the ground, creating an echo from both the crash and the shriek of pain from the creature. Midnight and Dream turned to see the wolf-like beast spread across the ground looking nearly dead, then looked up at me with expressions full of emotion.

"How did you do that?" They both said in harmony.

"I don't know. That strength took over again allowing me to do this I guess."

"Well, finish it off. We can't risk it staggering off and returning again for revenge."

No!" Dream screamed when she realize what Midnight was planning.

"Why protect it? It attacked us. It deserves this." Midnight walked over to it and grabbed it by its throat, raised it off the ground and held up his other hand to its chest as he prepared to administer the final blow.

"Let it go." I said as I stared directly into Midnight's bloodthirsty, revenge driven eyes. I grabbed his arm that was pressed against its chest and threw it down, then shouted,

"What do you not understand? Put it down."

He gave me a look of disgust as he realized he was the only one that wanted the beast

slaughtered. "Why should I?"

"It's already hurt enough. It's not going to come back. I can tell." Dream replied with

tears in her eyes as she grabbed Midnight's other arm.

"You two are weak. You're never going to complete our mission at this rate if you

can't even finish off a mindless beast. It wasn't going to spare you." He let go off the

creature, letting it slam onto the ground and without another glance back, he walked off

into the shadows. "Let's go."

"Dream. Stay away from him."

"I know Twilight."

We continued following Midnight's lead and looked back at the creature to see it

stand and stare directly into my eyes with feelings of both hatred and relief before it

jumped into the sky above, vanishing among the leaves.

"The next trial is ahead. We'll stop here to rest and allow you two to come up with a

plan besides 'harming' Dream." Midnight sat back against a large tree and closed his eyes,

leaving Dream and I to talk amongst ourselves...

The New Plan

Dream and I went off towards a more vacant area in the forest, leaving Midnight behind to think and allow us to talk in peace.

"Twilight. What are we going to do? There's no way I could gain control over whatever I was supposed to do. I wouldn't have a clue how to even get close."

"I know. But I'm not risking letting you get hurt just for Midnight and me."

"But what other choice do we have right now?"

"I'm not sure. I'll think of something...anything less dangerous for you."

"Well from what Midnight told us, we don't have much time left."

"I know." Silence filled the air as we both thought of something besides the current situation to discuss. Neither of us said anything or even made eye contact for a few the next few minutes, which in here for some reason felt like decades went by.

Dream broke the silence by asking, "How long do you think we've been in here?"

"I'm not sure. A few hours maybe. Why?"

"Just wondering. Didn't you say something about ghosts meeting you tonight or something?"

My face lit up when I remembered that. "I completely forgot about that. Maybe that will be the answer to our problems. I have to go off alone, Dream, if I want to make sure I come in contact with them again."

"Why?"

"Last time they came to me in a dream, or at least what I think was a dream, but this time I feel as though I'll see them in reality and for that to happen, I must go alone. Stay with Midnight. I know I warned you to stay away from him but at least for the time being he can protect you from anything unknown."

"How will I know you're safe though?"

"I have your good luck charm remember? Nothing bad will happen, I can protect myself."

"Fine." Dream stood up and turned away from me. "But I'm not happy with this plan, and I'm going to worry about you until you're back in sight."

I walked up to Dream and wrapped my arms around her from behind, hugging her tightly as I whispered, "As long as you're worried about me and care about me, I'll always be safe." She started to tear up and turned around to give me one of her signature hugs while hiding her face from me in attempt not to show me that she was crying.

"Just be careful Twilight. I don't know what I would do if I ever lost you."

"You never have to worry about that Dream." I whispered then gently kissed the top of her head and felt her loosen her grip around me. "I'll be back soon Dream. I promise." I motioned for Dream to go on, and I watched as she walked away, making sure she was safe until she reached Midnight. He looked up at me; he knew my exact plan just from the momentary glare we shared before I turned away.

"Now to find these two again and clear something's up." I said to myself as I walked off into the shadows, still envisioning Dream in my head and hoping for her safety the whole time. "Heh, I guess Dream means more to me than I ever thought she would."...

Hybrid Awakening

The darkness seemed like the perfect way to contact the spirits in reality without too much of a hassle. The demonic entity could easily manifest itself from the shadows surrounding and the more angelic one seemed to be able to flash itself in with ease. All I has to do was wait until they arrived so I could find out the answers I desired. I leaned against a tree and closed my eyes, attempting to sense their presences again.

A few minutes went by, which felt like hours in the solitude, and yet I still could not sense anything approaching from any direction. I stood up getting ready to go in search of them. Before I could open my eyes, an arm extended from behind me and wrapped around my throat, pulling me back against the tree and holding me there. "Think you're powerful enough to predict us," a familiar voice declared in my ear, "Think again." It let go and laughed as I dropped to the floor gasping for air. I turned to see the demonic spirit emerging from the shadows in the most sinister manner possible.

"You...you're here." I struggled to say through the pain of its grip.

"We both are." The angelic ghost said as it also emerged from behind the tree.

"As we said we would be. We are here to continue what needed to be finished."

"Yes. Now tell us Twilight, what do you need to know?"

"Well first, who, or what, are you?" I asked as I finally stood up face to face with them again.

"I am known as Abyss." The demonic one answered.

"And I, Illumina. And as for what we are, we are parts of you, the part that control your darkness and light for now."

"Yes, each time you've needed us, or have been endangered, we've taken control and finished whatever you couldn't handle on your own."

"But how do I get control of my own powers without your help?" I asked both of the spirits.

"We shall explain that momentarily, but for now you need to beware of the dangers you will face ahead."

"This will be the last time you will see us, and the last time we can save you, so you better learn how to unlock your strengths quickly or it'll end badly for you."

"You mean...?"

"Yes. We are going to show you how to unlock our abilities willingly and from that point on, you're on your own." Abyss explained.

"Now to start, clear your mind of everything and focus solely on your inner strength." Following what Illumina said, I closed my eyes and cleared my mind, but I could not sense anything within me that they said would be there.

After a few seconds, Abyss seemed to grow impatient as he growled and said, "Hurry this up already. What's taking you so long?"

"I don't know. I don't feel any inner strength within me."

"Well then, now it's time for my method," Abyss said and finished with a demonic laugh. With that, it rushed at me, wrapping its clawed hand around my throat and impaling its claw into the trunk of a tree, leaving me no space to move and little space to breathe. Then he lifted his other arm and quickly motioned it towards my forehead, slamming the back of my head against the tree hard enough that it felt as if my skull cracked. It let out an echo of pain that seemed to spread throughout the forest, filling the air momentarily then vanishing. "Open your eyes!" I stared into his terrifying eyes and lost complete feeling in my body as if he were draining me of my energy. "Don't look away!"

I could feel my body getting weaker with each passing second as I gazed into its monstrous eyes. I soon felt as though my consciousness was slipping when suddenly, a rush of energy spread through my body, giving me a familiar feeling of strength and yet this time I was in control.

I raised one leg, bent it against the tree like a spring, and used it to push upward while using my other leg to attempt to strike Abyss's arms and break free. Instead, it let go before the impact succeeded and jumped back toward the shadows, yet I could still see it through the shroud. Using the momentum from the releasing movements, I leaned forward, completely in the air, so that for a split second I was standing against the tree before I pushed off, soaring toward Abyss. I attempted to grab onto him but he ducked, letting me fly above, He attempted to swing up into my ribs, but before he could, I grabbed onto its hood and used my speed to toss him and sent him crashing into his original hiding spot.

He jumped up and bent low, similar to the way a tiger preparing to pounce, and ran at me on all fours in a fit of rage. "It's over." Illumina said as it appeared between us, grabbing Abyss and pulling it back inches before its claws could reach my face. "You've awakened the strength for him already, enough is enough."

"No! Now this is personal!" Abyss roared as he attempted to break free, but Illumina seemed to have a stronger grip than either of us expected.

"Abyss, you can't win. Look at his eyes, their complete. The more you fight, the more you'll hurt your own pride." Abyss let out a thunderous roar that spread across the forest then calmed down and stepped away.

"What do you mean by my eyes? What's happened to them?" I asked eager to find out since Midnight mentioned the same thing.

"Rather than looking the normal way they do in your calm state, you've unlocked your hybrid eyes, which are filled with pure black with a white center." Illumina explained. "Soon you'll awaken every possible technique, but for now your strength and agility have been enhanced tenfold."

"And now you're in control and can do so at will." Abyss added.

"What do I do now?"

"Return to the others, and focus when you can to unlock your next level of abilities." Illumina said in a soothing manner.

"Oh, and as a parting gift, we'll give you your first weapons. You'll need them."

"What are they?" I asked in curiosity.

"The last remains of us." They both declared, and before I could ask what they meant, a brilliant light shone from behind them, blinding me momentarily. As I shielded my eyes, I could see them both forge their bodies into two separate, unique items. As the light faded, both Illumina and Abyss had formed two dagger-like blades, one that was pitch-black with a blood red handle, and the other a radiant white with a blue handle. I picked up both blades and examined them, the black one having a jagged edge similar to fangs made for tearing, while the white one had a smooth, sharp edge made for slicing.

"Abyss and Illumina. You two will aid greatly in the upcoming battle." And with that, I slid each blade into the pockets of my jeans and turned back, heading to reunite with Dream and Midnight. "Nothing will stand in my way from this point on."...

Illusionary Awakening

Getting back to Dream and Midnight seemed easier than when I was leaving, as if I could see through the darkness. My eyes changed, to the point where the darkness seemed to have faded, allowing some light through and for me to see with ease. Making my way back to Dream and Midnight, I began to wonder how we could awaken Dream's power without causing her harm, either physically or emotionally. Before I could think of anything, I was reunited with Dream and Midnight who were now both asleep. I walked over to Midnight first and woke him, letting Dream rest while we tried thinking of a plan.

"Midnight. Wake up." I said as I nudged his body making him fall to his side.

"What happened?" He woke up in a momentary daze as he scanned the area.

"I've done it. At least somewhat I have."

"What do you mean 'somewhat'?" He asked while he stood up dusting off his clothes. Before I could even respond, he looked up at me and saw my eyes then smiled and said, "This is definitely good news. Destiny is back on our side."

"Yeah, sure. Now let's talk about Dream."

"What about her?"

"What's the plan for awakening her, without hurting her physically or emotionally? I'm not going to let anything bad happen to her so we have to think of a better idea than that."

"I've got another idea, it's similar but won't cause any damage and will save us time and energy."

"Yeah? What is it?" I asked curiously. He leaned close to me and whispered an idea that was insane but had a great possibility of succeeding while following my rules.

"You understand?"

"Yeah." I responded. "Let's get this over with."

While my eyes were shut, I could feel two presences nudging me whispering next to my ears. "Dream..." I heard Twilight say and then a tap on my arm that I guessed was him waking me.

"I didn't realize I fell asleep." I said mid-yawn as I stretched my arms and rubbed my eyes.

"It's okay, but we have to move. That thing is back." He explained in a worried voice.

"Where?" I asked as I realized what was happening.

"In the bushes, it hasn't spotted us yet but I saw it. Midnight went on ahead, we're going to meet them. Now let's go quickly." He pulled me up to my feet and grabbed my arm making me follow him faster before I could see that creature.

"Where are we going?"

"Into the illusion, it won't be able to follow us in there."

"Are you sure?"

"That's what Midnight told me before he went ahead." I could see a bright wall of light ahead as we approached.

"Is that it?"

"Yeah." We ran into the wall of light and ended up in what looked like Twilight's resting place.

"How is this possible?"

"I don't know, it's an illusion I guess and it's playing our memories against us. But we can't wait, it's still behind us."

"But...I thought you said it won't come here...." I began to panic as I thought of that monster attacking us again.

"That's what Midnight told me. He must have been wrong again." He paused as if thinking of how to explain something. We stopped running and he turned to me, "I've got a plan. You stay hidden and I'll get rid of that beast again. I did it last time so I should be able to again." He smiled at me in an attempt to reassure me but I still felt worried for his life. "We don't have time to waste, go over by those bushes and hide."

Listening to what he said, I ran over to a large section of bushes with enough shadows to hide, but still allowed me to see what was happening with Twilight. I laid on the floor under the bushes and watched as Twilight stood there staring into the forest ahead of him, awaiting its arrival. It dashed out of a bush at Twilight and he moved to dodge it but not fast enough as it tore a gash into his arm. It took everything I had to prevent me from running out to help him, but I knew if I did, I would get in his way killing both of us. A feeling of emotions swarmed within me as I feared for his life.

A second time it pounced at him and caught him off guard, slashing a scar across his chest and tearing through his shirt and jacket. The feelings became harder to control as I covered my mouth to prevent myself from making any noise. A third attack came as it charged Twilight but this time he grabbed it by its arms, freezing it in its track, saving himself from what would have been a deadly blow. He pulled it in closer then spun around, lifting it into the air as he did, and tossed it into a tree a few inches away from me. Rather than being harmed, it used the tree as a slingshot and fired itself right at Twilight. Not expecting the attack, it slammed into Twilight and forced him back against a tree with such force that the entire tree shook and a cracking sound echoed through the forest. I thought it was the tree cracking from the impact but as I looked closer, I realized it was the sound of Twilight's ribs breaking from the crash. With Twilight still in its grip, it held him pinned against the tree, and I heard him whisper, "Dream..." as he coughed up blood, then his head dropped and his body hung motionless.

"Twilight!" I screamed as I realized what happened. A feeling new to me grew within me as what happened registered in my mind. I ran at the creature screaming at the top of my lungs, tears running down my face. My eyes blurred from the tears and it seemed as though the world was melting away, including Twilight's motionless body and the monstrosity that did that to him. "What's going on?" I mumbled as I slowed down and looked around. I heard Twilight voice say, "She did it," and I turned to see him and Midnight standing behind me unharmed.

I looked back at where Twilight was before and saw nothing but a few bushes and trees spread around the area. "What's going on?" I asked, "And what is this strange feeling I have?"

Twilight ran at me and hugged me, lifting me off the ground and whispered, "You did it. You awakened your hybrid." He kissed me on the cheek gently and let me back down onto the floor as I stared up at him. "You broke the second trial on your own, using your powers through your own self-will." He declared with a smile. I stood there silent, just staring at him. "What's wrong?"

"What's wrong...?" I whispered mimicking him, "You let me believe you died just so I'd unlock my stupid hybrid form."

He was shocked by my reaction and stood there silent, showing signs of remorse growing in his face. "I'm sorry. It seemed like the only way..."

"Whatever. I don't care." I responded as I turned my head. He looked down at the ground and before he could continue I wrapped my arms around him and gave him the biggest hug I could. "I'm just glad you're really okay, Twilight. You don't understand how scared I was thinking I'd lost you forever. Please..." I became all choked up as I tried to finish talking, "...never let anything happen to yourself. I can never lose you like that."

"I already promised you, I'm never going to leave you here alone and I'm your protector, so you have nothing to worry about..."

"I don't need a protector!" I screamed at him, "I need a...never mind" Midnight stepped forward, now close enough to hear everything being said as he stared at us wondering when we would finish.

"No. What do you need?"

"Nothing, let's get going. Midnight is waiting."

"Okay...but you're telling me once we get out of here."

"Sure." I said as I thought to myself, 'I don't need him to protect me, what I truly want is for him to care for me the way I feel about him...for him to love me.' We continued walking and Twilight lightly tapped my hand before holding it as we walked and whispered "So I'll never lose you," and smiled at me.

I leaned up and kissed him on the cheek and said "Thanks." and I watched as his cheeks lit up with a light red blush. 'Maybe he already does'...

Misery and Hope

"What's next Midnight?" I asked as we searched for a clue of how close we were to the next trial.

"This part is completely unexplored, so I wouldn't know what has to be done to pass the final test. My guess is it will have to do with either your powers or my own since Dream's trial is passed and one of ours is completed."

"Well if it is my turn, then this will give me a chance to test out my control over this new strength and possibly allow me to unlock more secrets hidden within." We continued walking along what seemed to be an endless path in silence for the next few minutes. I looked at Dream to see if anything had changed about her since she awakened her abilities but she looked exactly the same, although when Midnight was in his hybrid form, his appearance was different than it is now. "Dream, do I look any different to you?"

"No, maybe a little more serious but you still look like the same old Twilight to me."

"What about you Midnight? You noticed a change in me before, so do I look any different?"

"No. You've returned to your natural state."

"Natural state?"

Midnight took a deep breath as he fixed his glasses and tried thinking of how to explain a natural state. "Basically, a natural state is how you are normally without any hybrid influence. When you use your hybrid form your appearance, as well as your abilities, are changed to distinguish the difference between the two forms. A hybrid experiment, that being us, goes back to being in their natural state from doing so on command, after being a hybrid for an extended period of time, or through exhaustion. If your body can't handle any more and all of your endurance is drained, it automatically returns to your natural state in an attempt to conserve some energy to keep you alive."

I noticed Dream was attentively listening in on the whole conversation as well, seeming both worried and interested by the new information. "What do you mean to keep us alive?" She asked as soon as she gained the courage to.

"Although it greatly helps you at the moment of need, using your hybrid form also drains your energy quicker than expected, leaving you exhausted at a faster rate. Dream, you would know better than either me or Twilight because you've reached your limits before and once you do, you faint. Twilight, I believe you've also experienced that feeling after your first encounter with Hybrid Dream." I stood there silent as I thought back to that moment, remembering the level of exhaustion I was at after that battle. "The problem we soon will have to face will be the battle we soon will engage in."

A jolt of realization shot through Dream and I as we both realized the risks of that face off soon to come. "Our lives will be in danger when that time comes." Dream mumbled through her daze.

"Yeah, and we will have to know as much as we can about our enemies before that time comes and train our bodies beyond their limits if we wish to survive."

The rest of the journey remained mute as we continued through the little remaining forest until we reached a barren wasteland with what looked like a canyon dividing the land. Far on the other side stood a monstrous building that took up most of the horizon and as I grew closer I realized what it was. "That's the factory from my nightmares and visions!" I screamed as it came more into focus.

"It is!" Dream agreed in the same manner.

"Well, there's only one thing left until we find out our answers...crossing that canyon."

I looked down at the abyss and thought to myself 'this isn't going to be easy.'...

𝔄 𝔕isk 𝔚orth 𝔗aking

Staring down at the darkness of the abyss, I tried to think of a way to get across this bottomless pit. The distance is twice the length any normal human could jump, maybe more, and the idea of climbing down and scaling the opposite side is out of the question when the base of this gorge was hidden in a veil of shadows. The unknown led to thoughts of horror and misery as I realized how many failed attempts to get through these trials and the many attempts made to get to that massive building ahead just to see what mysteries reside deep within its confines.

"Twilight." Dream said lightly, snapping me out of my daze and bringing me back to reality. "How are we supposed to get across that?"

"I'm not sure," I turned to Midnight who was also staring into the darkness below, "Any suggestions?"

"Not exactly. I'm not sure if I have enough control to bring the three of us over safely and the risk is too great to take without considering other possibilities."

"What other possible methods are there?" I asked in a sarcastic manner.

"Give me time to think." He mumbled back in a rude manner as he stared down at the ground.

Allowing Midnight to be in solitude as he thinks of other strategies, I moved back by Dream, who was lying on the floor staring at the sky above. "Isn't it unbelievable how within this short time we went from being normal people to 'destined' heroes according to Midnight?"

"Yes, it definitely is. I never would have believed this to be true if I didn't see it through my own eyes." I joined her and lay next to her, staring up at the mysterious night sky.

"Twilight?" She whispered as she turned towards me.

"Yes Dream?"

"I'm sorry for hurting you, even if I wasn't in control." I looked into her eyes, seeing

a great amount of remorse in her stare as she tried hiding her feelings from me.

"Don't worry about it. I'm fine, aren't I? I knew my Dream wouldn't really hurt me."

She smiled and moved in closer, leaning against my arm and gently whispered,

"Twilight's Dream? I like that." and smiled as she stared back up.

"What did you say Dream?" I asked as if I couldn't understand her while I slowly

wrapped my arm around her.

"Oh, nothing." With a smile, she looked up at me again, this time with eyes full of joy

and bliss. I pulled her in closer, holding her tighter in my arms as she laid her head upon

my chest, listening to the gentle melody of my heartbeat as she slowly shut her beautiful

eyes. Lying on my chest, she looked like an angel bringing hope to this journey of

nightmares.

"That's it!" I shouted, disturbing Dream's rest as I stood up and walked towards the

forest we emerged from.

"What do you mean?" Dream asked with a puzzled expression on her face as she

stood up.

"I can't explain it; it's just something I have to test." A lie. I could easily explain my

plan but I knew Dream would refuse to let me test it if she knew how insane it was. I

backed up until I was as far away from the canyon as possible without any obstacles dodge.

I waited a few seconds, channeling my energy from within until I felt a full control of my hybrid swelling within my body.

"Your eyes...?" Dream declared in a nervous tone, "What are you planning?"

"Just watch and you'll soon find out." With that I charged full speed at the gorge and dove directly in.

"Twilight!" Dream screamed at the top of her lungs.

"What are you doing?" Midnight yelled in a tone more furious then worried as he watched me plunge into the abyss.

Both of them ran up to the line where I jumped to see what was happening. An expression of both shock and amazement appeared on their faces as they saw me hovering with my new hybrid ability.

"You're...flying?" Midnight remarked as he watched me rise back from the darkness.

"It looks like my idea was true." I said with a smirk as I looked to my left and right sides. Two wings emerged from my back, one similar to those from Abyss and the other the same as Illumina's wings.

"But how?" They both asked in harmony.

"I got the idea from you Dream. You made me think of an angelic spirit I saw and reminded me that they had wings, so I decided to test if I could as well." I landed in front of the two of them and Dream first slapped me across the face with all the strength she could gather at the moment, and then rushed me with a hug. "You're so stupid! You could have died! What if that plan didn't work?" Tear filled eyes stared directly at me as she awaited a response from me.

"I guess I was just so sure it would work."

"Well we're lucky it did." Midnight stated as he moved in closer. "It looks like we can get across now. You take Dream, I'll use my power to manipulate space, creating a path

for myself and we will meet on the other side."

"Sounds like a plan. Don't do anything stupid." I demanded in a joking manner,

which was quickly dismissed when both gave me a look of disapproval. I picked up

Dream, carrying her in my arms, and made my way across the gorge as I stared at Dream.

'She's so beautiful, everything about her is amazing. I can't believe she cares so much

about me' I thought to myself as we nearly reached the end.

She looked up at me, catching me staring at her and said, "What are you thinking

about Twilight?"

"Oh, nothing." I responded with, and with a whisper I included, "Dream. My love."

Whether she heard me or not, I didn't know but at that exact moment she wrapped her

arms around my neck and kissed me on the cheek, making a smile spread across my face as

we landed on the opposite side. I lowered her legs first, allowing her to regain her balance

as we remained abided for Midnight, who seemed to be nowhere in sight. The only thing

that was visible was a faint flash of light then darkness yet again...

𝔖𝔢𝔭𝔞𝔯𝔞𝔱𝔦𝔬𝔫

In an attempt to reserve stamina, I forced my body back into its natural state as we awaited Midnight's arrival from across the gorge. Time slowly passed and yet he still remained hidden from our sight.

"Do you see him?" I asked Dream as she focused on the path, searching for our teammate.

"No. Do you think he's okay?"

"I'm not sure. He should have been here by now." I awakened my hybrid eyes to try searching through the veil of shadows for him, but even with that, I could not see him anywhere in sight. "Did you see a flash of light before?"

"Yeah, what was that?"

"I'm not sure," I released my hybrid eyes to prevent reducing my energy any further and turned to Dream, "I think whatever it was has to do with Midnight's disappearance."

"What could it have been?"

"Maybe another attack, I'm not sure to be honest." At that exact moment, what looked like a fireball flew between Dream and I, so close that the air it passed through was burning every part of my body, sending a sensation of pain through my veins momentarily. "What was that?" I screamed as I saw another faint light flash, this time headed directly at us. I pushed Dream aside and dove to the ground, just narrowly dodging the second flaming sphere as it flew overhead. "We have to move! Now!" I grabbed Dream's arm and ran towards the enormous building ahead.

"What's going on? Where are we going?" Dream questioned in a panicked tone.

"We're going to take shelter in that building; whatever is after us won't be able to find us in there." We ran through the destruction and searched for a place where we would not be found easily. A chill filled the air, cold enough that our breath was visible, making it difficult to remain hidden. A shadow passed, alerting us that we were not alone in this monster of a laboratory.

"Dream." I whispered while watching the shadow's movements in the other room. "When I say to, we're going to make a run for it into that door over there. We can't stay here, we'll be found too easily."

"Okay."

"One...two...three!" We both dashed from behind some unused equipment and made our way to a large metal door on the opposite side of the room. I grabbed the handle of the door and pulled as hard as I could, opening it just enough to squeeze through silently. I went through first to inspect the unknown area and motioned for Dream to follow through as well. She moved forward when a loud crash of glass echoed through the silence surrounding. Dream looked down, saw a shattered syringe under her sneaker, and tried to ignore it and continue towards the door. Without any warning, the door slammed shut before Dream made it through, trapping her with that unknown creature. I used all my strength that I could gather to push the door that now barricaded me away from Dream, but as I struggled, the metallic sheet between us grew hotter by the second. I backed away from the door, noticing it glowing a bright red and orange as the heat welded the metal to the walls surrounding, permanently sealing us apart.

"Dream!" I screamed but no response, making my mind flood with imagines of horrible outcomes of Dream trapped with that creature alone.

I turned to search for an exit to this storage facility and noticed another small wooden door on the far left side. I made my way towards the door when I felt a shift in the air that gave me the feeling I was not the only one in here. As the feeling grew, the temperature of the room seemed to drop to the point where I was shivering uncontrollably. As I pulled the door open, a breeze blew past, slamming the door back shut. I turned to see the silhouette of a young girl standing among the shadows watching my every movement with a large smile on her face.

"Finally, you're here." the mysterious girl said and stepped out the shadows...

𝔄 𝔠𝔬𝔩𝔡 𝔖𝔦𝔱𝔲𝔞𝔱𝔦𝔬𝔫

As she emerged from the shadows, the temperature rose back to its normal level without cause. As she moved closer, I could see that she looked young, maybe around sixteen or seventeen, and was wearing light blue, ripped jeans and a tight, long-sleeved black shirt. On her wrist, she wore a bracelet with white snowflake designs that linked together, glistening in the light with each step. She was fair skinned, with big blue eyes and blue hair that looked like something a pixie would have.

"Who are you?" I asked as she crept closer.

She reached out and grabbed my hand, wrapping her small, soft fingers with mine as she stared into my eyes. Her skin was ice cold even though the room we were in was warm enough to heat anyone up. She leaned in close to me, with her lips right next to my ear and whispered, "My name is Dawn, and I know all about you Twilight." Her breath sent chills down my spine as she gently brushed my neck with each word she said.

"How do you...?" Before I could finish my question, she put her hand over my mouth, and moved in closer, pressing her body against mine and forcing my back against the wall.

"Relax. I'm not going to hurt you." She said with a smile on her face. With her hand still covering my mouth, there was nothing I could say. My body was frozen as I tried to move away and failed with each attempt. She pulled on my shirt, forcing my head lower and with a sudden movement, kissed my lips softly as she wrapped her arms around my shoulders. She took my arms and motioned them around her waist then slid her fingers gently up my back until she reached my shoulders where she let her arms rest.

With a motion of her smooth, icy lips, she made a simple, childish peck into an intimate situation as she pulled my body closer. As the moment escalated, she raised her hand and ran her thin, delicate fingers through my hair and in almost a fluid motion; I raised my arm to her face and caressed her cheek while lightly brushing her skin with my fingertips. She slid from my lips, lightly kissing me down my cheek and onto my neck, sending a sensation through my body, making me shiver with each touch of her lips. With each passing second, the feeling grew unbearable as she continued to motion her lips against my skin in ways that drove me crazy.

"How does that feel?" She whispered gently between each soothing motion.

"A...maz...ing." I struggled to say through the chills she sent down my spine, leaving me breathless.

She pushed her body tightly against mine leaving no space between us, sending a piece of glass from above tumbling down onto the ground shattering into a million pieces of glittering dust. The sound of the glass woke me from my trance as I remember Dream being trapped on the other side with some unknown and dangerous creature. I pushed Dawn away, holding her by her arms just far enough away that she could not reach me as I said, "I'm sorry, there's someone I have to find right now."

"Who?" She said with a hint of jealousy in her voice, still being restrained.

"Someone who means everything to me." I said as I pictured Dream's smiling face in my mind. "I can't do this with you. I'm sorry."

The hint of jealousy grew to an envious glare as she stared at me. "Is it that Dream girl? What's so special about her? I'm ten times the girl she will ever be. She could never do the things I can do for you. Stay with me."

"No. She's..." I struggled to say the word as I realized what Dream meant to me, "my love."

"No! I won't allow that! I'm the only girl for you." Her voice echoed with fury as she struggled to get loose from my grip. She closed her eyes and when she opened them again, they were a bright snow white rather than the blue they previously were. Her hair gained streaks of glistening white through each section and her body temperature dropped instantly, freezing my hands and forcing me to let go. "You will be mine Twilight. You don't have a choice."

I moved closer to the door and slammed open the door, pulling it shut behind me before Dawn could get through. I held the handle on the door as tight as I could as I heard Dawn approach the door and felt a tug as Dawn tried to get through. The handle began to get colder by the second and before I let go, I grabbed a bar from the floor and forced it through the handle, jamming the door shut. I backed away, noticing the handle began to glisten as if it were covered in an icy coating.

I rushed down the hall in search of Dream, hoping she was still alive and that I could get to her before either Dawn or that creature. "Nothing will stop me from saving you Dream. I'm going to keep my promise!" I yelled as I ran down the narrow path noticing a door at the end. I tackled through the door, sending it smashing into the wall with an echo loud enough to attract anyone's attention, both good and bad...

𝔄 𝔥𝔢𝔞𝔱𝔢𝔡 𝔒𝔲𝔱𝔠𝔬𝔪𝔢

"Twilight..." I whispered as I realized the door was forced shut, "Twilight...help me."

I was alone. In a room with an unknown enemy that was after us. I backed into the

shadows of the room, trying to remain concealed until Twilight returned so we could

escape this nightmare together.

A sound came from outside the door, footsteps growing closer, a shadow projecting

through the doorway. A man appeared in the doorway, attracted by the sound of the

syringe as he scanned the room for the source. He walked up to the door, placed both

hands against it, and seemed to be focusing to gather some hidden strength. The door

began to glow bright shades of orange and red as if it were melting under a massive source

of heat.

With the light from the glow, some of the feature of this unknown person became

visible as I tried to remain hidden from his sight. He looked similar to Twilight physically

but with crimson hair that had orange streaks through it, and seemed to have the eyes of

an inferno as he stared at the molten metal. He wore a black hoodie with tribal flames that

ran up his back to the top of his hood, along with a pair of black jeans that were scorched

in some areas.

Realizing my hiding spot was being lit up as well as his location, I slowly crept from

the wall to the door he just entered from hoping to escape before he finished what he was

doing. As I grew closer to my destination, I felt relieved that I was lucky enough to remain

undiscovered this entire time.

"You're not as sneaky as you think you are." He turned from what he was doing,

staring directly at me through the shadows I remained hidden among, as my heart pounded through my chest. With each step that he took towards me, horrible images of what he would do to me when he reached me flashed through my head.

Only a few feet away from him, I made a run for the door hoping I was close enough to make it through before he could reach me. I reached the entrance but at the same moment, he grabbed onto my arm catching me before I could get out completely. His hand felt like it was burning a hole throw my skin as his grip increased and the distance between us closed. Terrified for my life, I panicked, pulling as hard as I could to get away, but to no avail. Within my state of fear, a feeling of power filled my body, giving me hope as I turned to him, staring directly into his burning vision.

"What are you trying to do?" He said as he stared into my eyes, then he began to look worried as his grip loosened. "What's going on? What are you doing?" He let go of my arm and dropped to the floor, covering his eyes as he yelled in horror at what he was seeing. I used this chance to my advantage to make my escape into a separate area where he would not find me.

"I guess my illusions really do work well." I said to myself with a smile as I ran through a door that left me in a long, seemingly endless path with two choices to choose from on which way to go. "Now to find Twilight." I made a left and made my way down the hall until I reached an unlocked door at the end. I ran inside and crouched behind a few crates that were lying around, hoping whoever that was did not already start his search for me.

A few seconds later, the door flew open and smashed into the wall it was latched to, sending a roar through the room as a figure stood in the doorway, his face concealed by the darkness.

"Please no. Don't tell me he found me already." I whispered as I began to panic once again...

Reunited

The door flew open and hit the wall with such a great impact that the hinges holding the door in place screeched and cracked, nearly letting the door collapse onto the floor. As I entered the darkened room, the feeling I was being watched swelled within me but from where was a mystery.

"Who's in here?" I said aloud, not considering the fact that Dawn or that creature could have somehow gotten in here through a hidden passage.

"Twilight..." I heard whispered from behind a stack of crates. I walked closer to where the voice came from and peered around the crates to discover Dream balled up on the floor staring up at me. "Twilight!" She stood up and hugged me as tight as she possibly could.

"Are you okay Dream?"

"Yes, now that you're here." She said with a smile. "What happened to you?"

"I ran into a new enemy, but I escaped and trapped her far behind." I paused as I thought to myself, 'I can't tell Dream what else happened...that would devastate her.' "What happened to you?"

"The same. He seemed to manipulate heat and fire. He's the one that sealed that metal door shut and his touch nearly burned my skin. I narrowly escaped using my illusions, but I don't know how long that will hold him off." And with that, an explosion from behind seemed to express her point. We both turned to see that through the broken door, a fire ignited one of the hidden passageways in the hall and through the blaze emerged a man. The door I exited from shattered as well as if frozen, revealing Dawn as she passed through in a fit of rage.

"That's her!" I yelled as I pulled Dream's arm to help her up.

"And that's him!"

"Come on, we have to move!" Pulling Dream along with me, we ran through a glass door that seemed to lead to a vault with no other exits.

"What are we going to do? We're trapped."

"I...I don't know. Search for an exit or some way out." We both scavenged through the room in hopes of finding some sort of exit, but every possible passage out was boarded up with wooden planks to prevent what was originally in here from escaping.

"There is no way out Twilight. They're getting closer too! What are we going to do?" She screamed as she stared through the entrance, watching our two enemies draw closer. An explosion from behind us sent a section of the boarded up windows crashing down into pieces of rubble as something flew through the destruction, slamming into a collection of lab equipment, shattering it all. As it emerged from the demolition, I realized it was Midnight, his clothes torn and his body cut up from what seemed like an intense battle.

"Midnight. Where have you been?" I asked as I helped him climb out of the remains of the shelves.

"There's no time for that! We have to move!" He roared in a fit of fury.

"But where? We're cornered in here."

"This way. Twilight, get over here. I need your help." He said as he pointed to what looked like a window that was covered for safety precautions. "Help tear down this barricade." With that, we both ripped off a plank one at a time until we could make our escape.

"Dream. Go first, then you Midnight. I'll go through last." Following that order, Dream passed through with ease, and then Midnight made his way through with no problem as well. I turned to see Dawn and the man Dream mentioned entering the room, as well as another guy climbing over the debris from Midnight's entrance. I began to climb through the hole when I heard a voice say "Where do you think you're going?" but before they could reach me, I dropped out the passage, slamming into the ground below. I ran toward the canyon where we originally arrived here, reuniting with Midnight and Dream on the field surrounding the laboratory.

"Use your hybrid forms quickly and get across that gorge before they catch up!" Midnight barked as his body changed from its natural state. I focused and this time it was easier to awaken my hybrid, with my wings extending as well. I grabbed onto Dream and began to glide across the crevice as I watched Midnight run across as if the land never ran out. I followed Midnight to the edge of the forest where we stopped and hid among the trees. "We should be safe here." He whispered as he tried to regain his breath.

"That's what you think." A blonde haired horror said as they appeared a mere twenty feet away from us.

"How did they get here?" Dream yelled as she noticed they were on our side of the canyon.

Ignoring her question, I stepped forward, revealing myself in the light as I stared at the three of them. "Who are you?"

"I'm known as Pyre. I guess you could say I'm the leader of this group." The crimson haired one said as he stepped forward.

"I'm Dawn as you already know." Dawn said with a smile that hid her true personality.

"I'm known as Pulse. You're friend over there has already met me personally." He had long spiked, blonde hair with light blue tips on each hair along with blue and yellow eyes that showed his psychotic manner with every glance. He wore a saffron sleeveless shirt, ebony cargo shorts, and a necklace with a lightning bolt as a medallion.

"Together, we are known as Fusion." Pyre continued, "And we are your destruction." Before I could respond, the three of them ran at us at full speed.

"Twilight, you can't win. Not yet, we have to retreat." Midnight yelled as he stepped out from behind the trees.

"But how? They'll keep following us." At that exact moment, a blur charged passed me and rushed Fusion. It was that beast from earlier that we spared. It pounced at Pyre and attempted to attack him, knocking him back onto the floor as he struggled to get it off him. It gave us the distraction we needed. We ran through the forest as we escaped the new menaces that threatened out lives. I turned back to see Pulse holding that creature by its throat as Pyre place his palm on its chest, igniting its body as it let out a shriek of pain and terror...

Retreat and Recover

We fled as quickly as we possibly could for what felt like hours as we made our way through the pitch-black forest. The obscurity of the darkness made the forest seem like a perpetual labyrinth as we dodge through trees and bushes, making our way back to my haven. The three of us continued through, no one uttering a single word until we reached a familiar area.

"We should be far enough away by now to have lost them. At least for the moment." Midnight explained as he stopped in a patch of light. He did not turn to face us, but instead just stared up at the bright sky with his fists clenched at his side. He walked toward a tree and leaned his head against it, then without reason swung his fist into the tree, chipping some of the bark and leaving a crack in its place.

"What happened back there?" I said as I moved in closer to him.

"What do you think happened? We were ambushed by those three abominations. Those were the enemies we were created to destroy. As you can tell, at this level of strength we're clearly no match for any of them." He paused and took a deep breath then finished with, "At least I'm not."

"What happened to you?"

"That maniac Pulse or whatever his name was attacked me from a blind spot, catching me off guard while the other two went after you. We had what felt like a never ending battle outside of that building and at first we were at even strengths, but as I grew weaker, he seemed unfazed by the damage of the battle."

"How did they know we were going to be there?" Dream asked as she thought about the trio.

"Who knows? Maybe it was planned, or maybe it was coincidence. But that doesn't matter at this point. What do you know of the other two?"

"That girl, Dawn, seemed to have some sort of control over ice and had similar changes as we do when she tried to harness that power."

"And Pyre seemed to manipulate fire." Dream added.

"And Pulse, from what I experienced, possesses lightning," Midnight explained.

"This can't be real. It just doesn't make sense, Project Hybrid, Fusion, destined battles, otherworldly powers, it just seems too fake, almost like a horrible nightmare." I mumbled as I thought of the situation, trying to come up with some logical explanation for all of this.

"Well, you're nightmare is a reality. This is real; we can't deny it out of fear. The world has many unknown phenomenon, but that doesn't mean because it's never been seen before that it isn't real. Now we have to prepare for what will soon come and train our bodies beyond their limits. We'll also need a strategy." Midnight remarked.

"What do you mean a strategy?" Dream whispered as she thought of training methods.

"As you've seen, together those three easily took down your little pet back there. We would not be able to defeat them if they are all together. Our best chance will be to separate them and take them on individually. That also means we have to enhance our solo fighting abilities and awaken our hybrids completely. This is not going to be a simple task and it will lead to complete exhaustion as we train."

"Then we don't have time to waste. Let's get started."

"Remember the element they control when training. Pulse is mine, I owe him for that cheap attack and I'm getting my revenge this time." Midnight declared with a bitter

tone.

"I'll take on Dawn; she's the only girl so that should even up the standards."

"And that leaves Pyre to me. Sounds interesting." I remarked.

"Let's get rest and being training immediately at sunrise." Dream said with a

cheerful tone.

And with that, I walked to my old resting place and lay down to get some rest. As I

closed my eyes, I began to envision Pyre as he stepped forward, revealing himself as the

leader of Fusion. If that is true and from what Midnight said in the past, I'm the leader of

Project Hybrid; this will be a duel of the ages between the leaders of two destructive

forces...

Cimmerian Rebirth

As I lay down, I could not help but get the overwhelming feeling of terror as it coarse through my veins. 'How am I supposed to get stronger and awaken my hybrid when I hardly know anything about it? Two days ago I was just some outcast who didn't know anything about himself and now I am supposed to somehow jump into the role of leader and face off against any enemy force that obviously has more control and strategy with their powers.' I didn't sleep much that night, trying to come up with a plan that will allow us to work together or a training method that would give me control of my elements. I took out the blades formed from Abyss and Illumina, holding them above me as I hoped somehow I would get a sign for what to do next.

The forest seemed as though it too were asleep, along with every living thing within it. Little movement occurred, the occasional windblown bushes and leaving vibrating in the breeze were the only sounds. I began to get the feeling that this was the peace people talk about before a devastating storm. And Fusion was that storm soon to come.

With no solutions coming to me directly, I searched my surrounding for something that might assist me in my thoughts. The serenity of the night allowed the perfect atmosphere for walking through the night, considering my possibilities. I watched as the nocturnal animals made their way through the obscurity, in search of food. A lone wolf emerged ahead of me, staring directly at me with eyes as black as night. Its fur was a darkened silver, with an ebony striped running down its spine. It was larger than most wolves that wandered this area, and seemed more sinister as it stealthily made its approach towards me.

Rather than approach as a predator, it advanced with a cautionary manner resembling that of a well-trained hunter. The mysterious creature was logically planning

each of its movements perfectly, instead of trying to attack at any moment. This abnormal

wolf was unlike any that existed before, and for some reason I felt like it had something to

do with me.

Once it was within a few inches of me, it raised its head focusing its sight directly at

my eyes, and for a moment, I felt as if it were peering into me, with a strange connection

that felt as though we were one. As if perfectly timed, the moment I thought "give me a

sign that this is true' it let out a mighty howl that broke the silence of the forest. I ran my

hand down the spine of this great beast, and more of a connection grew within me.

I saw another vision of the laboratory as it once was, before Project Hybrid reached

its final stage. "This magnificent specimen will do perfectly doctor. With it, hybrid will

evolve beyond human weapons, and will expand to even greater capabilities."

I looked at what these scientists were discussing and in a containment center was a

young wolf, unconscious and suspended in some liquid.

"This lone wolf was located in the forest surrounding our lab. Some how it got

through the defensive precautions we set up and made it closer than any unwanted visitor

has done before."

"It will fit perfectly into my experiment, and it shall be known as Cimmerian. It may

be a great use to our newest hybrids."

"Hopefully this one will be a success, and not another failed attempt that loses all

sense of control like the last one."

"Ah, but with every fail, comes a better understanding of what must be done. And

our last attempt works perfectly as a guard dog for the first stage." And with that, both scientists let out a maniacally laugh.

Awakening from this vision, I looked down at the creature as it gazed at me with a stare that showed it understood I knew what it was.

"Cimmerian. You may be more of a help to us then even your creators assumed." I turned and walked deeper into the forest as my new partner, Cimmerian followed shortly after. "I will not let what happened to the last beast happen to you. Not this time..."

Shadows of My Mind

I returned to my resting teammates, with the two of them both still asleep as they regained their strength for the upcoming battle. As much as I knew I should be doing the same, I could not bring myself to fall asleep. All that had been happening lately seemed to be hitting me directly now, not giving my mind a chance to rest. Although my body was sleep deprived, I felt fully awake and energized, as if I already slept through the night. Is this one of the effects of being a hybrid, having all of my limits extended, including the amount of sleep necessary to function?

I looked back and forth between my comrades as I considered their abilities and the possible strategies that could be used during this war. As a pair, each of us can work together well, with several different combinations, but as a whole, there were no plans that would work without risking one or all of our lives. Every scenario that played through my head ended in horror as one of us ended up brutally injured or even killed. And Fusion obviously has no remorse for the lives they have taken, especially since they could easily torch that beast without a second thought about it.

'It seems as though one on one battles better the odds, with Pyre as my target. The combined powers of darkness and light versus the intensity of fire in a clash of leaders. This will be the most difficult trial of my life so far, but I can't allow myself to fall victim to his strength. I have to win for the sake of my team and to protect the lives of everyone that I hold dear. Especially Dream.'

'With the assistance of Abyss and Illumina, and the unknown abilities of Cimmerian on my side, I will not allow myself to fail.'

I held the blades forged from the spirits who kept me alive this far and tightened my grip on both handles as I clenched my fist. A wide range of emotions ran through me as I

thought of the fight, ranging from excitement to test these mysterious abilities to pure

terror at the thought of risking my life. I stared up at the moon high in the sky as I realized

the night was coming to a close. And with dawn's arrival, the search for our new enemies

shall commence.

The bright shine of the moon projected a shadow across the ground that was hidden

from me just moments ago. Yet this shadow seemed so unfamiliar to me, as if it did not

belong to me. As I watched my silhouette slowly faded in and out as clouds obscured the

light, I noticed something beginning to happen. It seemed as though the shadow was

fading less and less the more I focused on it and it seemed to become more solid and

darker each passing second.

At first, I thought my eyes were playing tricks on me because of my exhaustion,

because the shadow began to rise from the ground and form its own body. The shadow

formed its own shape, forming that of a human body and yet with skin as dark as the night

sky. It rose to its feet, and remained still as if awaiting an order.

It opened its eyes and from them, a white pupil was exposed with a light variation in

the darkness surrounding its eyes. It had eyes similar to the ones Illumina described my

hybrid eyes to look like.

"It seems as though I have a new trick." I said as I stood face to face with my shadow

copy. "This should put the odds in my favor," I said with a smirk and then it vanished, and

the bright lights of sunrise spreading through the trees. "It looks like it's about time to

move out." I declared as I stared at the rising sun...

Return

The sunrise, bright and awakening, slowly lit up the sky in a way that symbolically gave me hope in this mission but increased my horror within. In a way, the sun symbolized this situation, and just as it rises through the night sky, we will rise through this battle and be victorious. The negative aspect that sent chills down my spine is the sun, a flaming sphere, cuts through both the darkness of the night and the light of the moon, overpowering both and eliminating them for the time.

"Twilight." Dream whispered from behind me as she gently awakened from her peaceful slumber.

"Yeah. Are you well rested?"

"Yes, what about you?" She mumbled as she rubbed her eyes, keeping the bright sunlight out of her vision.

"I got enough yeah." Even if I did not sleep the entire night, I learned a lot of new information that will help in the end. I hoped.

"Where's Midnight?" All I did was look up and he came soaring down, landing between us, standing perfectly just as a cat would if it came crashing down from above.

"I hope you're all well rested. We need to move, I'm getting the feeling our little friends are close by." Midnight stated as he put his glasses back on after a night's rest.

"How close do you think they are?" I asked, although I felt more excited about it than worried.

"Within a half mile radius, maybe closer." He raised his arm and pointed his finger towards a path in the forest that became clear with the light of the sun. "In that direction."

"That's the town!" Dream screamed as she realized where he was pointing. "We have to hurry before anyone gets hurt."

"I'll lead the way; I know this area better than anyone else." I shouted as I shifted into a position to run. "Follow me." We hurried through the forest, I navigated us through trees almost instinctually after all the practice getting to my haven at all times of the day and night. As we drew closer to the city, the smell of smoke and ash filled the air, giving the feeling we were already too late. With only a few feet left until we emerged from the trees, I braced myself for the worst, hoping we made it in time to save the lives of some of the innocent citizens.

However, as the city came into view, my fear grew as we witnessed the destruction caused by Fusion, with the three of them directly ahead, waiting for our arrival...

𝔗𝔥𝔢 𝔅𝔞𝔱𝔱𝔩𝔢𝔤𝔯𝔬𝔲𝔫𝔡𝔰

The city, usually filled with cheerful people and large building, was now deserted and destroyed. Building were demolished, rubble covered the streets, fire spread across the streets burning every living thing in its path. Bodies on men, women, and children were lying on the floor, either burnt beyond recognition or frozen. It was a horrific site to gaze upon and in front of all of it stood Pyre, Dawn, and Pulse without any look of remorse on their faces.

Pyre just stood there, leaning against a wall with his eyes shut as if nothing happened. Dawn was lying on the remains of a wall staring up at the sky, completely ignoring our presence. But the most horrific appearance was Pulse as he sat on the corpse of a burnt civilian, staring at Midnight with the expression of a blood thirsty animal.

"Look's like they made it," Dawn said as she sat up and jumped off the wall.

"Finally, I can have some real fun." Pulse declared with a baleful look on his face.

"Well, shall we get started Twilight?" Pyre asked as he stepped forward, walking towards me.

"One thing first. Let's move the battlegrounds away from the city so no more innocent people get in the middle of this."

"Sounds good to me. Where would you like to go?"

"The field. Where we originally met. Any objections?"

"Let's go then." Pyre closed his eyes, seeming to focus and within an instant, an aura of flames emerged from his back, spreading through the air around him. The flames molded into a fiery pair of wings, resembling the wings of a mythological phoenix.

"Impressed?"

Before I had a chance to respond, he took off into the sky and flew over our heads with a glistening trail following his movements. I ran towards Dream, lifting her in my arms, and exposing my hybrid wings, following Pyre as I slowly gained on him. After a few seconds, I caught up with him.

"Ah. This shall be entertaining then." He remarked with a smile on his face. And with that, we raced through the sky within a few feet of each other, heading towards the battlegrounds of this monstrous carnage...

The Battle Begins

We touched down to the ground and I lowered Dream back down as we awaited the rest to make their way to the destination. An ongoing silence remained between the three of us that seemed to last forever. I took the moment to analyze Pyre in hopes of finding some weakness I could take advantage of but with little effort. All I could tell is that he had a relaxed persona, as if he did not have a care in the world.

"Pyre."

"Yes?"

"Who are you? And why are you part of this? You don't seem anything like those other two."

"It was not my choice. I was forced into this position."

"Do you remember what happened?"

"All too well. But that doesn't matter Dan...I mean Twilight."

"What did you call me?"

"Forget it. They're here." I looked up to see Midnight, Dawn and Pulse emerging from the forest ahead of us. Midnight walked behind Dream and the others followed Pyre.

"Are you ready for this Midnight? Dream?"

They both replied "Yes," although the sense of fear could be noticed in Dream's response. Midnight seemed filled with hatred towards Pulse and the look in his eyes clearly showed his craving for revenge.

"Hey Midnight. Don't do anything stupid." I jokingly demanded.

"Don't get yourself killed without a fight." He responded.

I revealed Abyss and Illumina and closed my eyes as I focused my energy. As I opened my eyes, my hybrid form awakened along with my teammates. "Get ready," I

paused for a moment to take a deep breath, "Let's go!"

I ran towards my rival with my weapons drawn, clashing my blades with his weapon,

a long, narrow sword radiating with the bright orange glow of the sun as sparks flew

through the air...

Darkness Is My Sword

The clash of our blades sent a gust of wind across the field, bending the trees nearby as our strengths collided. I struggled to force him back as he pressed forward, locking us in place. I used Illumina to push away his blade and knock him off balance, while swinging Abyss directly at his chest, it's tearing teeth inches away. He curved his body dodging my blade as it tore through his hoodie. He jumped back and stared down at the ripped cloth hanging from the shredded remains.

"This should be interesting," he whispered as he removed the hoodie. "Now let's get more serious." I removed my jacket as well to prevent any restrictions of my movements. "Before we continue this, let me introduce you to Cinder. My blade can harness the power of fire as it tears through my enemies one by one."

"And these, Abyss and Illumina, will be your downfall."

A shriek of pain caught my attention as I searched for the source. I watched as Dream collapsed to the ground. "Dream!" I ran towards her but as I grew closer, a wall of fire rose between us.

I glared back at Pyre and watched as he shook his head and said, "That's not your fight Twilight. I'm your opponent." He ran at me with his glowing blade slicing through the field, leaving a shining trail following each step. The heat from his weapon could be felt before it reached my body as I attempted a sneak attack with Abyss again. He countered it by catching my wrist mid-attack. "You call this fighting." He stated with a laugh.

"I don't see you doing any better."

"Then so you shall." His blade ignited in flames as he forced through my defenses, slashing through my shirt and burning my skin. I screamed in pain as I felt every nerve the blade encountered being burnt rapidly. In the midst of his attack, Cimmerian arrived, pouncing at Pyre. He tackled Pyre onto the ground, pinning him down as he attempted to tear at his throat. "So you have a pet? Well so do I!"

Pyre kicked Cimmerian off him, sending Cimmerian rolling across the ground as he tried to regain his balance. As Cimmerian returned to his pouncing stance, Pyre released a large flame similar to that which created his wings, this time forming a different figure. The figure grew legs from a narrow body, a tail extending from the end of it, and a crimson mane that encircled the sprouting head. Its eyes were horrifying, and the appearance of emblazoned claws and fangs extended from the nearly complete body. This great beast completed its transformation with an echoing roar that thundered like that of an erupting volcano.

The beast charged at Cimmerian and clashed as they tore at each other. The two were equally matched, with no sign of a predominate victor.

"Now that your little pet is preoccupied, shall we continue?" Pyre took into the air and dashed towards me with incredible speed as he prepared for an impact. I met him halfway in the air with Cinder and Illumina clashing and Abyss slashing his chest within the momentary collision. We continued passed each other, stopping a distance away as I stared at my opponent.

"Looks like this won't be so easy for you after all." I declared as he held his wound, shocked that he was hit.

"It seems you are correct. It looks like I'll have to fight without holding back."

"Neither will I. Now the real battle shall begin."

Illusions Are My Arrows

"It's just me and you, Dream. Prepare yourself." Dawn declared as she readied herself for battle.

"I won't lose." I said to myself as I focused my energy, "I promised Twilight I would not fail!"

"Then let's begin. I hope you don't disappoint Twilight." She said with a sarcastic smirk on her face.

The temperature in the air around dropped rapidly as I awaited her first movement. My breath became visible and chills ran down my spine, even with the wall of flames close by. 'Is this the power she emanates even before battle? This is going to be more difficult than I thought. And to make matters worse, I haven't grasped my Hybrid powers to their maximum yet.'

As the temperature decreased, small shards of glass began to form around her and with each passing second, their size doubled. The enlarged frozen crystals encircled her entire body, creating a wall of ice that seemed impossible to break through without a very fine weapon to pierce between the cracks. Without warning, a section on the wall raced towards me with such speed that it was impossible to dodge completely. Before I could react, a void opened in front of me encasing the shards and vanishing inches away from my body.

"Stop playing around! Take this seriously!" Midnight screamed from a distance as he watched my movements and lowered his arm.

"Thank you." I whispered as I realized he saved my life. "He's right; I need to take this serious." I closed my eyes and felt as the world around me began to shift and mold in the form of my imagination. "Now it's my turn." I opened my eyes to see a completely different terrain in which the battle would take place.

"How did you do that?" Dawn shouted. "What is this?"

A new sense of power coursed through my veins, a sinister, demonic strength that wanted control. I felt a new person awakened within me, ready to finish this battle in my place. "This is my domain. You will not escape from here as easily as you presume."

Dawn released another wave of crystals but before the impact could reach its target, a massive boulder emerged shielding my body. I raised one arm and held my hand out as a bow formed in my palm. It was large with brilliant shades of red, purple, and blue designs covering the limbs of the bow with a shining silver bowstring running between the two. I raised my left arm, pulled the string back and within my fingertips, an arrow appeared, with a black shaft and golden feathers.

I released the magnificent arrow and watched as it easily pierced through the boulder and left a clear path through Dawn's protection, slightly cutting through the tips of her icy blue hair. "The next one won't miss." I declared as she stared at me in awe.

"Not if I get you first. I have millions of crystallized beauties, while you can only launch one arrow at a time."

"Ah that's where you are wrong." I pulled back on the silver string again, but this time a bundle of arrows appeared within my hand, and from each arrowhead emerged two others, creating trident like arrows. I released and watched as my arrows shattered her frozen shield, removing one of my nuances. "This will finish you." I drew back the string one final time and whispered, "Nightmare, finish this," then released an arrow that sliced through the air.

Inches away from its target, the swift movement of a whip encased in icicles broke it in half, sending the fragments of the arrow crashing to the ground.

"You think you're the only one with tricks." She declared with a smile. "This is not nearly over."

Release

Within the second, Pyre was back on the offensive, his focus on a direct hit with no chance of allowing me to dodge. I used Abyss to catch the blade within its jagged teeth, momentarily locking it in place. Pyre thrust his blade through the grip of my dagger, narrowly missing my torso as it slid through the teeth of my blade.

I stepped back as the blade passed by my body, slashing it down with Illumina as I gained distance between the two of us.

"What's wrong Twilight?" He growled as he grew closer, "What happened to all that fierce talk just a moment ago? Have you given up already?"

"I'm just getting started."

"Well then fight as if your life depended on it! Stop kidding around or you will die here and now!" He stopped his pursuit and closed his eyes as he lowered his blade. "I'll just have to force the power within you out." He held his right hand directly ahead as sparks began to ignite in his palm. A flame grew within his fingertips, forming a sphere as he grasped the ball within his palm. "This should inspire you to fight."

The fireball shot from within his hand at me with an incredible speed. I had no choice but to take the blast in a defensive pose as I crossed my arms across my chest and lowered my head. The impact sent a wave of pain across my body, scarring my arms and burning the areas of my chest unprotected. The strength of the impact knocked me back, causing me fall onto one knee.

'I can't fool around anymore.'

I raised my head, focusing all my attention upon my fierce rival as I returned to my feet. "Ah, there's the look I've been waiting for, pure hatred and anger." He laughed in a maniacal way, similar to the laugh made my Midnight previously.

"So you want hatred? Then you'll have it." Ignoring the burns, I lifted into the air and soared directly towards Pyre with Abyss and Illumina ready to tear through his body. A feeling ran through me as I felt a new strength awakened. Our blades collided, forcing him back as I pushed forward with all my strength. "I will not lose!" My blades began to shine as my rage increased.

A voice began to call to me, 'Release the power.' That statement kept repeating through my head, echoing in familiar voices. 'Release the power.' The world was drowned out by the voices. "Who are you?" I screamed, throwing Pyre off guard.

"What are you talking about?"

'Release the power!'

"How?"

I pulled back on my attack, my blades still radiating a mysterious glow as Pyre gained his balance. "Now's my chance!" His screams sounded like a whisper among the voices.

"Release!" I screamed as Pyre swung his blade. A wave of energy expanded from the shining daggers, forcing Pyre into the air and separating the battle between Cimmerian and the beast summoned by Pyre.

"What was that?" The voices vanished, only leaving Pyre shouting in rage and confusion. Astonished by this new power, I decided to test its abilities in battle. With a single slash of Abyss, an ebony ray glided through the air, only slightly missing Pyre.

"So the real battle begins." Pyre said with a grin.

"This fight is over." I combined the power of Illumina and Abyss as I slashed toward

Pyre, creating a cross of darkness and light. 'There's no way he can dodge this.' I thought to myself. 'It's over.'

Pyre raised Cinder in both hands and as it began to shine above his head, a surging inferno emerging from the blade, colliding with my attack as the two lit up the sky. 'The victor of this fight may not be so clearly determined. I know what I must do'...

Maniacal Laugh

"Ready to die? I won't go so easy this time." Pulse declared with the look of murder in his eyes.

"Last time wasn't a true test of my power, it was an ambush. What are you going to do without your boss to help you this time?"

"Oh, you'll see how powerful I am without the limitations of Pyre."

"Then enough talking and let's begin this!"

"My pleasure!" His eyes began to shift to a golden shade along with variations of blue streaks emerging within his blonde hair. 'I can't hesitate this match.' Gathering all of my energy, I entered my hybrid form with just enough time to brace for the first impact. His speed was faster than the others, mirroring his element of lightning as he charged towards me. Every movement was a flash, teleporting side to side as he grew closer balling his fist ready to attack. His punch landed within my grip as I defended myself, but the look on his face proved he planned for my reaction.

"It won't be that easy." I stated as I held back his attack.

"Wrong move." He shouted with a sinister smile, and then his fist began to shine brilliantly and burn within my grasp. A jolt of electricity channeled through his body into my own, forcing me to release him as the pain overwhelmed me. I backed away, feeling almost paralyzed in both arms when I heard Pulse begin to laugh. "This is too easy." He raised his fist and swung it directly into my jaw, causing me to collapse to the ground. His laugh continued even louder, echoing through my head like nails on a chalkboard. "I'll finish this now." He raised his fist and with a smashing force brought it straight down towards my chest.

The impact on the ground formed a crater, creating a dust cloud surrounding Pulse. "It's over." He proudly rejoiced.

"I warned you not to underestimate me without your little leader to defend you."

"Who said that?" He screamed blindly into the dust. He dropped to the ground to clearly see the shattered earth under him when he noticed his target had vanished. "Where did you go? How did you do that?"

"I control time and space, you expected to defeat me that easily." I began to imitate his maniacal laugh, "No sir, it is you who will die here." I placed my palm on his back and sent a shockwave that forced Pulse to glide though the air until his body crashed into a tree.

As he fell to the ground, he stared up at me and whispered, "How? You were paralyzed, how did you escape my attack."

"That would be too complicated for someone as blockheaded as you to even contemplate. I'll save you the misery and finish you off here with my method of choice." I raised both arms overhead with my weapon materializing within my grasp. "Crescent Apocalypse. A beautifully crafted, dual-sided crescent blade connected by an indestructible chain. With this in my hands, I have never lost a battle, and to prove that I'll finish you with it as well. Goodbye Pulse."

I swung the chain overhead until it gained enough speed to hold itself in the air and released it toward Pulse's injured body. Halfway through the air, something collided with it knocking it off course, just narrowly missing him. "You talk too much. You gave me enough time to bring about my 'method of choice' for stealing the lives of my victims as well. However, I won't explain it in as much detail as you did. All you need to know is that your death will be brought upon by Discharge."

He used to tree to regain his balance, catching his weapon in his right hand. It looked similar to a large golden shuriken in the shape of bolts of lightning. He spun in a circle before releasing the shuriken, giving it an extra boost of speed as it hurled towards me. I used the chain of Crescent to defend myself before the weapon could hit its target. It dropped to the floor in front of me as its circulation ended, useless from this point. "Great weapon." I said in a sarcastic manner as I pulled back upon my blade.

Without saying anything he held up his hand and as the shuriken rose and returned to his grip, ready for another attempt. "Impressed."

"I'll finish this before that weapon even touches me." As I yelled, a pain coursed through my body. I looked at the source of the pain where my arm was bleeding through the jacket. 'How is this possible?' I stared back at Pulse just in time to see him catch the shuriken once again. 'When did he throw it? And how did I not see something that large heading towards me.'

"Before you even ask, consider this. How fast does lightning travel? To give you a simple answer, faster than you can dodge." He began to laugh once again. "What was that threat before? You'll kill me before I even touch you? What happened to that?"

"This won't be so easy. I'll have to use that method, although it will greatly decrease my energy to the point of body failure. But I have no choice.'...

Visionary Duo

"Dream!" I yelled as I retreated from Pulse's assault. "I have a plan, get over here!"
She fired a few arrows from her new bow as a distraction before dashing to my side to hear
my plan. "This was the original plan that was thought of when we were created. Both of
our powers control aspects not visible to the human eye, unlike Twilight who controls the
powers of darkness and light. We were originally known as the visionary duo because both
of our abilities involve vision; mine involving what is seen and yours with deceiving. We
have to combine our efforts if we want a chance to win."

"How do we do that?" She whispered into my ear, making sure we could not be
overheard.

"To start, I need you to create an illusion that can occupy a majority of this field.
Leave Pyre and Twilight out of it, their battle is on a level far above ours." To prove my
point, the moment I said that a flash of light brightened the sky near the location of the
two indestructible forces. "You can see through your own illusions and I'll use my
technique to see through it as well. That will leave Pulse and Dawn trapped and we can
finish this before it gets too risky. Got it?"

"Yeah. When should I sta...?" Pulse cut her off before she could finish her question.

"Just to let you know, you chose a very poor plan already. As you can tell, Pyre is
well on his own fighting without us but the two of us have come up with our own method
of fighting to be equal to his power. The combination of our strength, known as
Stormbreaker, has never been defeated before and this will not be an exception."

"Do it now Dream." Suddenly, the world began to melt around us, with our leader
and his opponent vanishing into the sky. It was unbelievable how fascinating yet

destructive the power of an illusion can be. The trees in the distance, lively and full, were stripped of their leaves. Our surroundings darkened as an eclipse blocked the light of the moon, blinding everyone on the field. The air became thick and unbearable to breath as the wind ceased.

"What's going on?" Pulse shouted to Dawn as the distance between them grew farther apart.

"It's an illusion produced by that Dream girl. We have to break it quickly or this could get bad."

"Now's my chance to act.' Closing my eyes, I focused all the energy of my hybrid form into my vision, allowing me to use multiple techniques but drastically removing others.

While in his confusion, I swung my weapon at Pulse, landing a direct hit that caused him to collapse to the ground, blood dripping for his arms and torso. He searched for me yet I was invisible to him in this realm as I crept closer. I held up my weapon over his injured body and attempted to slam it down before I caught a glimpse of movement. Dawn swung her whip directly at me. I dropped to the ground, inches away from Pulse, barely dodging her attack. When I looked back at Pulse, he swung his shuriken, still in hand, toward my crouching body.

'How is this possible? I can't risk it.' "Delay!" His attack slowed enough to allow me to avoid the impact, only slicing through my clothing. "Dream, what's going on?"

"I don't know. They're getting through it somehow."

"Ah, naive little Dream. I won't fall for the same trick twice." Dawn said as she moved in closer. "I may not be able to see you clearly but my hearing remains unaffected by your little illusion. I can hear every move you make, as with your friend's." She swung

her whip, cracking the air directly between us with perfect precision. Pulse gathered

himself until he was back on his feet then made his way behind Dawn, whispering quietly.

"Now it's our turn."...

Infernal

As the collision faded in the sky, I soared towards the airborne Pyre with Abyss and Illumina at my side. A direct impact sent Pyre spiraling towards the ground, my pursuit shortly behind. Inches above the ground, he spread his wings to keep his levitation barely alive as he braced for my assault. A wave of debris scattered throughout the air as we collided, crashing against the earth surrounding us.

"Why are you doing this Pyre?" I screamed with fury in my voice. "What's the point of killing innocent people and targeting the three of us?"

Struggling to get the words out while defending, he began to mumble quietly. Then his eyes met my own as they shifted once again. "You'd never understand what I went through! I will get my revenge on everyone involved in those monstrous experiments, including you Twilight! I don't care who gets in my way, they're all worthless in my eyes." The center of his eyes began to mimic the shade of a burning flame, while the surroundings blackened. This was no longer the same Pyre, but instead felt like the eyes of an awakened demon.

"What happened to you?" I tried to force him back against the ground, but with little avail as this new persona took over.

"You want to know my story? Is that your dying wish? Then so be it." He broke the struggle with ease and created a wall of fire between us, lowering his weapon. "My family was slaughtered directly in front of my eyes, each one of them mercilessly. I was just a child at the time and could not defend myself as it all happened. Terrified, I left the site of my family's murder. Before I realized it, I was completely alone, with nothing but my hatred to fuel my motives. I soon discovered these incredible powers, and set my target on everyone that was involved in the torment I had suffered."

"But why target us? Why those innocent people back there? What gain comes from pointless murders when none of us have a thing to do with your past?"

"That's where you are wrong. You were created as my enemy. I was created to defeat you, and that means you're in my path to vengeance. If I don't kill you now, you'll soon appear again in my path. It's easy to remove of you three before that time comes."

"If that's your motive, then I'll just have to stop you here and now."

"I was refraining from letting it get to this point but it looks like there is no choice. I'll have to awaken him once again."

"Who?" I shouted as a cynical smile spread across his face. He raised one hand and covered half of his face, maniacally laughing the entire time. He let out a shriek of pain and dropped to his knees, lowering his head to the ground. "Pyre?" His body began to tremble, his palm still covering a section of his face. Using this momentary vulnerability, I charged towards him, slicing through the wall of flames between us as I stood over his collapsed body. I raised my blades over his head and with all my strength, brought them down as hard as I could. A cloud of dust enveloped the area, hiding my target and leaving me unaware if I succeeded or not.

Then the laughing began again, and from within the veil of dust I heard his whisper, "Too slow little Twilight. You're going to have to try a lot harder to kill us." His voice vibrated with each word, as if two people were speaking at the same time.

"Us? Where are you, Pyre?" A sharp pain struck my ribs as I noticed a direct kick that knocked me out of the cloud. Before I could react, he was above me, fists raised over his head as he slammed them directly into my chest. Spiraling towards the ground, he appeared below me with his blade held above him ready to impale me.

Spreading my wings, I narrowly missed the blade's edge and gained some distance between the two of us. He was still staring into the air where I was with his blade over him, like a statue frozen in time. "He's fast. This is unbelievable. How did he get this powerful in seconds?"

"We've always been this powerful foolish child. Pyre is weakened by his emotions but we are not." A smile spread across his face that showed the demonic creature within Pyre. His eyes were blackened, similar to the description of my own by Abyss, but with blood red centers that sent chills down my spine. He slanted his head towards my direction and with a psychotic look shouted, "We are Infernal!"

𝔖𝔲𝔡𝔡𝔢𝔫 𝔇𝔢𝔞𝔱𝔥

"We cannot allow them to create a plan Dream! We need to finish this soon before things get out of hand!" Looking towards the battleground Twilight and Pyre were occupying, I could see each brought the battle to the next level as Twilight soared across the sky attacking Pyre without his blades in hand. 'It seems as though this is getting to risky, Twilight is not supposed to reach that level unless he is losing complete control.' "Dream. Twilight is in danger. Before you say anything, listen to me. We have to end this battle now and join him before he loses his identity."

Dream stared at me with a seriousness I had never seen in such young eyes, and faced our opponents ready to end the battle. "Let's finish this then. Before my emotions for Twilight take over." She drew another arrow and launched it directly at the injured Pulse, only slightly missing but stopping his movements towards Dawn. "What are you waiting for?!" Dream's anger fueled a new personality that would never be expected from such an innocent looking girl.

"Just make sure to know who you're target is." With that, I focused my sights on Dawn as she awaited another sound to know our locations. Using the same technique as used against Twilight, I dashed towards Dawn at a speed she could not track. Unaware of my movements, Dawn seemed frozen as she awaited the slightest sound to swing her whip at. I slashed at her with one side of my Crescent Apocalypse, keeping its other half nearby for defense. Within inches of the impact, Pulse's Discharge knocked it off balance creating a loud echo that spread across the field.

"That's it!" Dream shouted as a plan suddenly struck her. "Midnight, get over here quick." Dashing to her side, I realized she let her guard down and made enough noise for Pulse to hear her well enough to find her position.

"Dream! Look out." And then he appeared, the monstrous lunatic towered over Dream, covered in blood and scars, raising his arm across his body. He swung with full strength, directly colliding with Dream's already battered body. The way her body bent around his colossal forearm seemed impossible, as her spine twisted in half with a shatter and a twitch. She flew across the field and crashed into the ground, rolling to a stop without motion to her frame.

"One down." Pulse whispered as he stared at me with eyes no longer human. Those words echoed through my thoughts.

"How dare you? How dare you take the life of that innocent girl! Do you realize what you've done?"

"Oh I'm scared. Don't worry, you'll soon be joining her, along with your friend over there."...

Revival

Her body laid motionless for what felt like hours as our opponents stood together awaiting my next move. I tried to focus, to come up with a plan, but I could not get my mind to work properly after watching the gruesome scene of my partner's demise. It replayed through my head again and again, only fueling my rage as I screamed out her name. I charged towards the monster that took her life as he stood there, facing my direction but unable to see me.

"You monster!" I screamed, not caring if my voice revealed my location. "I'll kill you!" He swung his fist forward but missed as I ducked under his attack and tackled him to the ground. I held him down with one arm as I swung at his face with the other. Each hit knocked his head to the side as his body twitched under me trying to break free. His strength seemed to weaken as each hit continued, but a glow began to radiate from his body. Electricity shot from his skin, forcing me off of him as he rose from the ground.

I ran towards him again, but the electricity from his body created a barrier, protecting him from any physical attacks at a close range. "You really should not have done that." He whispered as he moved in closer. I backed away slowly, trying to keep distance from the bolt releasing from his body when a tightening grip wrapped around me. Dawn's whip encompassed my entire body, binding me still as Pulse continued his path. "Now, it's your turn." He raised his fist in the air as he did to Dream, and as he swung it forward a flash flew passed my eyes. Suddenly, an arrow struck his arm and he screamed out in pain, ending his assault.

I turned towards the direction of the arrow to see Dream standing in the distance, preparing another shot as he aimed for Dawn. She fired the arrow, forcing Dawn to release me from her grip as she dodged the attack. The two retreated as they realized what was happening.

"Dream? What's going on?" I questioned as she joined me, prepared to fight once more. "How are you alive?"

"I never died. That too was an illusion, to distract the two of them long enough to find an opening."

"Wow. You've mastered your illusions far more than presumed. Even I could not tell it was another trick." She fired an arrow at Dawn once more, clipping her leg as she stumbled to the ground. She seemed to lose her strength as she returned to her original state, lying still on the ground as she watched her comrade flee.

"Let's finish this." She whispered as we followed our opponents. "My power is fading." The walls of the illusion slowly deteriorated as her power decreased, allowing the two a path to escape.

"Forget that. They're finished, we need to help Twilight before it's too late." They watched as Pulse charged towards the two airborne demons ahead. "We can't let him interfere. Grab Dawn, she can't do anything now."

True Pain

"Prepare to die!" Screamed the possessed Pyre as flames engulfed his body. Within a flash, he appeared before me with his blade swinging upwards as a trail of fire followed its path. With little time to react, I used the rigged edge of Abyss to cease the attack momentarily as I gained some air and distance from this monstrous onslaught. This strategy seemed to work until the sound of Infernal's split voice behind me broke the confidence of my plan. "Too slow!"

Before I could turn to defend myself, his leg landed a direct impact across my ribs that sent my body spiraling across the air towards the pitch-black forest. "How could this be happening? How could this be the same guy I was just at a stalemate moments ago?" Balancing myself out in the air, I tried to brace myself for another attack but his movements were untraceable. Instantly, he appeared behind me. I turned to defend myself but it was too late. He swung his sword towards me, slashing his blade as it torn through my skin, blood seeping from the open wound on my chest.

"That's it. Bleed. Scream. Die." He shouted as he laughed with each strike he swung. "You truly thought you could defeat us! Ha. You are nothing in our presence. You don't deserve to even witness our power!" I blocked the swipe of his blade but the strength behind it was unbearable, as it sent me soaring across the sky.

"I need to do something." I whispered as my body hurled towards the ground. "I can't give up just yet."

"Above you!" His voice echoed as he appeared by my side, crashing his arm into my open wound. I screamed in pain as I collide with the ground, his arm still connected to my chest. "You've been a nuisance to us for far too long little Twilight." He wrapped his fingers around my throat, raising my body in the air as he tightened his grip. "Now, how to finish this? We could snap your neck, leaving you motionless instantly. But that would not nearly be entertaining for us. Maybe we should slice of every limb, one by one, as you slowly die within our hands." He raised his blade to the wound across my chest, watching as every drop of blood evaporated against the heat of his blade. The edge of his blade pierced deeper into my body as he forced it into the gash and charred the skin around it. I screamed in pain within every motion he made, but my body was motionless from the impact.

"Aw, no more fight left in you? That's no fun. I guess I'll just end this now." With a motion of his wrist, his blade tore through my body as a burning pain piercing through my skin. Blood ran down his blade, and dripped down my body as he released me from his grip. Laying in a pool of blood, I was motionless. My vision blurred, and I could no longer feel the pain that spread across my body.

'Dream. I'm sorry'…

Into the Abyss

"Twilight!" A voice echoed through the darkness. "Twilight!"

'What is that?...Who is that?'

"Don't give up Twilight! Fight on. You can't quit now! You promised!"

'Dream?'

"Get up! She needs you right now! Get up!"

'And...Midnight? What's going on?'

'You cannot defeat him on your own.' A voice whispered from within the shadows. 'You need my power. Accept it and you will defeat any enemy.'

'Who are you?'

'Accept my strength. Forfeit control and you can save them all.'

'I, I'll do it, if it means I can save them all. If I can save Dream.'

Slowly, it felt as though I was losing control over my body once again to an unknown force within me. The pressure from this destructive energy was unbearable as it forced its way to power. An echo spread through my body. A heartbeat. And another. My heart beat faster and stronger each second.

A burning sensation ran across my body, starting from my legs as two intertwining threads burned its mark across my body. 'The threads of darkness and light.' It travelled along my limbs and up my neck until the sensation ceased below my eyes.

My body began to trembling uncontrollably as these marks burned their way onto my flesh, wrapping around my arms and across my wrists. 'Accept the power of the abyss. Accept the strength of the Abyssal Light. Harvest the power within and you shall destroy all who oppose.'

"Abyssal Light." Sections of my hair began to change, with each tip darkened while the rest lightened to a pure white. I could feel another presence within my body trying to take over and end this battle as soon as possible. Each marking connected with my blades as they dissolved within my palms. Unable to release my weapons, the scorching liquid spread across my skin, wrapping around my hands, filling me with excruciating pain. I attempted to scream as the pain continued, but no sound came out. Blood dripped from my fingers as the metal engulfed my hands, forming gauntlets similar to the appearance of each blade. Each fingertip began to sharpen as drops of blood solidified, creating metallic claws that spread across my wrist and connecting with the burn marks.

My body rose as it continued to evolve, change into something never before seen. I held my hands out, opening and closing them as I adjusted to the new weapons as they finished the final transformation. Without controlling my voice, I stared at each claw and called out a name for each. "Radiance," I whispered as I tightened the grip of the white claw, "And Arcane." A new sense of strength swarmed within me. All the pain from the previous impacts seemed to vanish as my body restored itself. "Now. To finish this."

Infernal turned towards his enemy, staring in shock as a lifeless body rose once again. "That can't be possible. You should not be alive. Not a mere human. What are you?"

I took a step closer, shorten the gap between the rival powers as he questioned me.

"Don't ignore us?" He screamed as the flames surrounding him grew brighter. "What are you?"

My body appeared next to him, inches away as he stared into my eyes, unable to comprehend what was happening. I raised my claw and lunged it towards his chest, slightly missing as he dodged my attack. I swung my arm to the left, placing a direct impact against his body as he flew through the air. I followed, instantly ahead of him as he tried to slow his motion towards me. I tightened my fist and connected with his back as I forced him into the air.

I flew around his path and balled my fists together above his head, slamming down against his skull as he dropped back to the earth. He spread his wings once more and a wave a fire emerged from his body, cushioning the impact. He rose from the ground and let out a battle cry before taking off towards me. His wings expanded as the fire around his body burned, engulfing Cinder completely increasing its size and power. He swung towards me, but my body raised both arms, catching the blade within my hands.

"Impossible! You caught it in your hands!" I pulled Infernal towards me, raising my leg as I forced my knee into the side of his body. He shouted in pain but kept his balancing, returning with an equal strong blow to my right arm. He kicked away and spiraled around with his blade in hand, creating a shield of fire surrounding him. Struggling to catch his breath, blood dripped from his lips.

"This is unreal!" He charged forward when a jolt of lightning flew passed him. I raised my hand, crushing the bolt with ease. "Pulse! Don't get in our way!"

"You can't do this on your own! He's beyond you. Let me fight him. By your side or alone, you decide." Pulse screamed as he charged towards me. He threw him weapon towards my body, but Crescent Apocalypse deflected it slightly as it flew pass my head.

"Twilight! I'll cover you, just go!"

I ran towards Infernal, spreading my wings as I lifted off the ground. I could hardly track what was going on, my body simply acting on its own at this point. Infernal raised his blade, prepared for an impact when shock spread across his face. I shifted my wings, slightly flying over his head as I passed by.

'What's going on? Why didn't I attack him?'

And then my claw pierced its target. My blackened claw dripped with blood, emerging from the back of my enemy. Pulse coughed blood as he grabbed my arm.

"Pulse!" Infernal's voice spilt as it screamed for his comrade. I pulled my arm from his body, leaving a gaping hole within his chest as he dropped to the floor...

True Fear

Infernal stared at his fallen comrade next to me, without saying a word more than his name. His eyes shifted from the body of the former Fusion member towards me as he tightened the grip on his blade. A smile spread across his cynical face as he began to laugh. "Worthless." He whispered as he spread his wings. "He should have known not to interfere with gods. He deserved exactly what he got. But you, you shall die." His wings beat against the air as he took off once more towards me. I raised Arcane, blocking my vision of my enemy as he began to glow.

"Solstice." I whispered as a wave of darkness shot from my palm. Infernal raised his blade, slamming it against my attack as he attempted to cut through it.

"You think that simple attack is enough to finish me…" He screamed but stopped short as I grabbed his face with Radiance and forcing him into the air. He spiraled through the air once more, changing his target from me to my teammates. "Might as well even the odds. You kill my team, we'll kill yours." He screamed as he hurled towards Dream and Midnight.

Midnight braced for his assault as Infernal flew towards him, but Infernal bypassed the obstacle. His true target was Dream. I appeared between the two of them, raised my arms to counter his attack. He sliced through the air, his blade landing in my palms as it forced me back. I slid against the dirt as he continued to force his way through me. "Twilight!" Dream screamed as she watched the scene before her eyes. I turned and faced her, seeing the horror in her eyes as she stared at me.

'That's not fear of Infernal. She's scared of me. I can see it.' My arm swung towards her, pushing her away as I released Infernal from my grip. Her body skipped across the ground as she rolled to a stop from my push. 'What am I doing? That's Dream! Why did I just attack her.'

'She was in the way. She will always be in the way.' The voice echoed through my head as I watched the battle continue. Every swipe of his blade, every swing from my claws, it was viewed through my eyes but not my control.

"Twilight!" Dream screamed once again as she struggled to her feet. "You don't need to do this. You don't need to fight anymore. Just be yourself. I can't watch this anymore. This isn't you."

Her words echoed through me as I gained some distance from Infernal. "I don't need to let someone else fight for me! I can win this on my own!" I screamed as I dropped to my knees, struggling for control over my body once more.

'What are you doing? You need me if you want to win this fight!'

"No…I…Don't!" I raised my head to the sky and let out a howl, forcing my way back into control. "I can do this on my own. I don't need anyone to do this for me." I faced Dream as she stared into my eyes. "Stay back. I don't want you getting hurt. And, thank you."

"Did you forget about us?" Infernal shouted as he swung his blade towards me. I dodged his attack, and reappeared a few feet behind him. He turned to face me and waited as we both awaited the next move of our opponent.

The Final Technique

"I will not fail! I cannot allow someone like you to remain in this world, murdering innocent people, people you never met before in your life, for your own personal gain. I don't care what you have gone through, or what your purpose is. Who decided that you should choose the fate of these people? Who gave you that right?" screamed the newly awakened Twilight. The collision of each swipe of his blade against every slash of my claws echoed through the air with the intensity of lightning piercing through the sky.

"Why care for these people? They are mere insects compared to me, compared to us. Kill one, and another appears. It's all the same. We are the next generation, the next evolution. Survival of the fittest." Infernal's words only mirrored his cruel intentions, exposing the true monster hidden within Pyre. "And if you can't see that, you are just as weak as them. And I will erase you from this world along with every other human I do not see fit to live in my world. This is your final chance, cease this useless fight and join me, as my subordinate, or die here and be forgotten by the world." I remained silent, unable to respond to such a question. Infernal ended his assault, awaiting my response as he flapped his flaming wings. "Well boy? What is your answer? Will you replace Pulse?"

A smirk spread across my face as the question repeated in my head, shocking the waiting Infernal as he watched my every move. "You seriously think I would join you in any manner, or serve as your subordinate? You really are as insane as you look my friend. And you will see here why I am not, and will never be, you're subordinate. Here and now, this ends. Prepare yourself."

"Wrong answer." The intensity of the flames extending from his shoulders grew wildly releasing such heat the night sky began to swirl and rage with the fury of an oncoming storm. His eyes grew darker, the red centers now shining within the surrounding lifeless abyss as he let out a war cry before making his move. Infernal lunged forward, swiping his blade through the air, only missing by inches with each attack. Unable to find an opening, I could only defend against this onslaught of attacks, awaiting my chance to break the cycle.

A swing of the blade towards my rib cage allowed me to end his rampage, as I caught his weapon within the palm of my gauntlet, Radiance, and forced the other into his chest. The impact forced Infernal away, releasing his blade as he dropped from the sky. His body fell from the sky, crashing against the ground as it attracted the attention of the others nearby. The remaining member of Fusion rushed over to see to her injured leader as he lie their motionless on the floor. Still clenching his blade, I could feel the fire within Cinder forcing its way through my gauntlet. As I released the blade from my grip, a horrifying feeling passed over me, and the whispers of the beast confirmed my suspicion.

"You didn't think it was over that easily, did you?" My arms and wings were forced together against my body as this undying creature grabbed onto me. Struggling to break free, I saw his grin, dripping with blood as we both began to plummet from the sky.

"What's going on?" I screamed as I tried to break free from his bind, with little avail.

"Our ultimate technique, Lifeless Flame Transfer. It allows us to revive ourselves from a life-threatening situation using the flames within Cinder. Should have dropped it sooner, you naive child!" As he screamed his final words, we collided with the ground, creating an explosion that surrounded us with the earth below as a massive crater formed.

Every nerve in my body was screaming in pain as I lie there, my body overcome by the cost of the power combined with the force of the impact. Every bone in my body felt as if it were shattered, numbing my skin as blood dripped from every limb. The screams of Dream were slowly fading as my vision began to blur. I struggled to move, but could not find the strength to stand.

As I turned my head, I watched as Infernal lie seemingly lifeless once again only several feet from my body. The gauntlets and markings began to fade, returning to their former shape as Abyss and Illumina in my hands. Midnight rushed over to lift my head and aid me in my attempts to stand. "What were you thinking?" He screamed as his eyes filled with tears, "I thought you weren't going to die here! Isn't that what you claimed?"

Dream gasped as she watched in horror as Infernal rose once again, staggering to his feet to finish what he started. "It ends here."

I forced myself up, pushing Midnight away as I tried to stand, only able to raise one arm as I held Abyss. Struggling, I used the last of my strength to stand and use my last resort. A shadow began to form behind my rival, grabbing a hold of the damaged monster and holding him in place. I limped forward, holding one leg as I forced through the pain to move closer. "You're right, it ends here. For you."...

Twilight's Resolve

"This ends here. You were a worthy adversary, but I can't allow this to continue on any further." Infernal struggled to break free from the grip of my shadow warrior as it held him in place for the final strike. Every inch I moved in closer, my vision blurred more and the pain from the impact intensified to unbearable levels. "I can't fail now, I have to finish this."

"Twilight..." Dream whispered as she watched me more in closer to my opponent, tears filling her eyes. "This isn't you...You don't have to do this."

"What are you talking about, think of all the lives this monster has stolen simply to satisfy his own urges? How can I allow him to continue living when he didn't think twice about the lives he stole?"

"Because Twilight, you're not a murderer, you don't have to be like him. You can end this now, you've already won. Look at him." I stared up at my enemy, watching as the last of his strength diminished and his attempts to break free slowly weakened. The look in his eyes, no longer filled with hatred or anger, showed another emotion as they returned to their former appearance. Regret. The monster I fought above was gone and all that was left of him was an empty shell. He no longer had the strength of Infernal overpowering his body and mind, forcing him to fight for its entertainment. Pyre had returned, now completely in control as he stared up at me, our eyes meeting and in that moment it all came clear to me.

"Pyre."

"Finish me Twilight. Kill me so I can end this life of pain and join my family once and for all. Do it!" He screamed as tears streamed down his cheeks.

"No. This is over. I won't kill you, living is punishment enough for your actions."

"Do it now! I don't want to continue in this life anymore, I can't continue feeling so alone."

"But, you're not alone. Don't you realize that? You have Dawn who has been on your side from the start, and I will not end the life of such a worthy opponent. This was...fun." I replied with a smile on my face as I dropped Abyss and released him from the grip on my shadow warrior. He dropped to his knees, his head lowered to the ground as the tears dropped to the floor.

"Why? Why did you spare me? I wouldn't have done the same for you."

"That doesn't matter. I won't kill you, Dream's right, I'm not a murderer."

"Hmph, you truly are everything they believed you would be. Then know this, you will have to learn who to allow to live, and who to kill when the time is right."

"What do you mean?"

"In time you shall know it all. But for now, enjoy your victory. Do know this though, there is another experiment that lurks this earth, more ruthless and powerful than either you or I. And when he arrives, he will not be defeated easily. You will need complete control of your hybrid form if you wish to be a challenge for him. I can help you with that, in repayment for allowing me to live."

"And what do you get out of this?" I questioned as I absorbed the shock of what he just explained.

"I have a personal history with this menace, long before any of this started. I will be there to end this enemy's onslaught. Now, will you come with me to train?"

"I will."

"Twilight, no!" Dream shouted as she overheard the plan. "I won't let you go. Please don't leave me. I need you. I lov..." A simple kiss ended her fears as I held her in my arms.

"I'll be fine Dream. Remember, nothing bad can happen to me." I leaned in closer, my lips inches from her ear, as I whispered, "Never forget me, and when I return, you'll see just how much I love you". She stood there, quietly staring at me as my words filled her head.

"Okay, Twilight. I'll be waiting for you...please hurry back. And don't hurt yourself."

"You know me, nothing will happen." I replied with a smile that made all her worries disappear. She hugged me once more, a kiss on the cheek and a whisper of her love for me back, and then released me to continue on my next journey. I turned to face Pyre, who was now on his feet and awaiting my next move. "Now, let's head out and prepare for the oncoming battle." I looked back at my team, and watched as Dream stood by Midnight's side, smiling with teary eyes. Midnight nodded and raised his glasses, expecting the decisions being made. "Oh, and Midnight, when I get back, I want a rematch for that cheap shot in the forest." He laughed, and I turned back to Pyre, ready to embark.

"As you wish." Pyre replied and turned towards the sunrise as we made our move into the unknown...

Project Hybrid 135